Captain's barking intensified.

Hannah clawed at her attacker's hands, and his grip loosened. She managed a punch to his solar plexus. The man gasped as she crawled out from beneath him.

Before she could get to her feet, he grabbed her leg and dragged her across the dirt. Sharp pebbles pressed into her skin.

Her K-9 lunged.

"Get away from me!" her attacker cried out.

He reached for Hannah's neck, and Captain growled in response. She thrashed back and forth as she struggled to breathe.

A thudding noise caused the man to let go of her. Her assailant bolted to his feet. From the ground where she lay, she saw the silhouette of two men fighting— no doubt one was Trevor.

* * *

Ever since she found the Nancy Drew books with the pink covers in the country school library, **Sharon Dunn** has loved mystery and suspense. In 2014, she lost her beloved husband of nearly twenty-seven years to cancer. She has three grown children. When she is not writing, she enjoys reading, sewing and walks. She loves to hear from readers. You can contact her via her website at www.sharondunnbooks.net.

Books by Sharon Dunn

Love Inspired Suspense

In Too Deep
Wilderness Secrets
Mountain Captive
Undercover Threat
Alaskan Christmas Target
Undercover Mountain Pursuit
Crime Scene Cover-Up
Christmas Hostage
Montana Cold Case Conspiracy
Montana Witness Chase
Kidnapped in Montana

Alaska K-9 Unit

Undercover Mission

Pacific Northwest K-9 Unit

Threat Detection

Mountain Country K-9 Unit

Tracing a Killer

Visit the Author Profile page at LoveInspired.com for more titles.

Tracing a Killer

SHARON DUNN

LOVE INSPIRED SUSPENSE
INSPIRATIONAL ROMANCE

Special thanks and acknowledgment are given to Sharon Dunn for her contribution to the Mountain Country K-9 Unit miniseries.

LOVE INSPIRED® SUSPENSE
INSPIRATIONAL ROMANCE

Recycling programs
for this product may
not exist in your area.

ISBN-13: 978-1-335-63826-7

Tracing a Killer

Copyright © 2024 by Harlequin Enterprises ULC

Love Inspired
22 Adelaide St. West, 41st Floor
Toronto, Ontario M5H 4E3, Canada
www.LoveInspired.com

Printed in Lithuania

MIX
Paper | Supporting
responsible forestry
FSC® C021394

Behold, I will do a new thing; now it shall spring forth; shall ye not know it? I will even make a way in the wilderness, and rivers in the desert.
—*Isaiah* 43:19

For my beloved dog, Bart the nervous border collie,
who was my best friend for over thirteen years.
I'm so glad you were a part of my life.
I miss you every day.

ONE

From the moment she turned onto the causeway that led to the island where Antelope State Park was, a feeling of unease settled around Utah highway-patrol officer Hannah Scott. As if sensing the drop in mood, her K-9, a male Newfoundland named Captain, groaned from the back seat of the patrol car.

This anxiety wasn't about the job she'd come here to do as a member of the Mountain Country K-9 team. This was about the past, the tragedy that had happened when she was ten. Her stomach clenched as flat land, straight road and expansive sky stretched before her. Images of the mountains and trees were reflected in the lake on either side of the seven-mile causeway. Such beautiful scenery normally would have created a feeling of serenity in her.

Instead, she was having a hard time shaking the sense of dread.

The sun was low on the horizon. She'd already put in a full day with the highway patrol.

She gripped the steering wheel tighter and spoke out loud. "Come on, Hannah, focus on the assignment that brought you back here."

Captain let out a muted yip of support.

Saying a silent prayer that God would help her do the job she'd been given with the Mountain Country K-9 unit, she concentrated on her driving. The task force had been formed with members of law enforcement from across the Rocky Mountain states to catch a serial killer, dubbed the Rocky Mountain Killer. Ten years ago, three young men under the age of twenty, all members of the now disbanded Young Rancher's Club, had been killed in Elk Valley, Wyoming, on Valentine's Day.

The case had gone cold until recently. Three new victims, all from Elk Valley but now living in other states, had been murdered with the same MO—shot at close range in a barn. The new shootings had started on Valentine's Day, less than seven months ago. The murder weapon had never been found, but matching 9mm slugs had been located at all the crime scenes. The task force had narrowed down the suspects to two men who had motive. Ryan York's sister Shelly had committed suicide after being dumped by Seth Jenkins, one of the initial victims. It could be that Ryan saw Seth's friends as equally culpable. Because of the young men's reputations for using women and dumping them, Ryan's desire to right an injustice had spilled over to targeting other members of the club. Ryan owned a Glock 17, which could have been used in the shootings.

The second suspect was Evan Carr. His sister, Naomi, who had recently married one of the K-9 team members, had been the butt of a cruel joke ten years ago. When one of the members of the YRC, Trevor Gage, had asked her to a formal dance the club sponsored, Trevor's friends had ridiculed her saying she'd been invited as a prank. In interviews, Trevor had sworn that he actually had liked Naomi and hadn't intended it as a joke.

Hannah had read the transcript of the interviews the team had done with Trevor. She had no idea if he was telling the truth or not. Ten years ago, the members of the club were known for being troublemakers and having a love-'em-and-leave-'em reputation with the young women in Elk Valley. Why should Trevor be any different than the young men he'd run with?

She'd met her share of that type of guy. Her sympathy was with Naomi. In high school, a boy had invited Hannah to a dance, but he'd never shown up. The utter humiliation of having taken the time to get dressed up only to stand alone in a corner of the gym still hurt after all these years. The memory of the group of boys who sneered and pointed at her from across the dance floor was seared into her psyche. She'd been hurt by men in other deeper ways including being cheated on.

Her assignment seemed straightforward—convince Trevor, who now lived in Salt Lake City, to agree to go into a safe house since he was the most likely next victim. As if to confirm the team's suspicions, the Rocky Mountain Killer—or the RMK—a tall man with blond hair, had been spotted in Salt Lake recently. Most of the team were in Salt Lake, including the task-force leader, Chase Rawlston.

Trevor appeared to be working against his own self-preservation, though. He'd left his home in Salt Lake for a remote campsite on the island, causing him to be even more exposed. Members of the team had tried via phone to talk him into going into a safe house until he stopped answering their calls. Now, it was up to her to try some face-to-face persuasion.

She clenched her teeth. Men could be so obstinate about accepting help sometimes.

She shook her head. Some people were just hard to understand. She had Trevor's dossier with her. Transcripts of the interviews the team had done, background information and a photograph. Intense green eyes framed by blond hair peeking out from beneath a silver Stetson seemed to look right at her from the picture. Trevor was handsome, she would admit, but the story of his meanness to Naomi lingered in her mind.

Knowing how men were, she didn't believe that he had really liked Naomi, and she doubted he'd changed. Once a scoundrel always a scoundrel. Wasn't that what her own dating history had taught her? After so much pain, she'd given up on the possibility of finding love. Better to focus on her job and being the best auntie she could be to her nephew and niece.

As the miles clipped by, a new feeling invaded her awareness. The fluttering heart and shallow breathing indicated fear. Glancing off to the side where the Great Salt Lake was, she found herself struggling to take a deep breath. There was a reason she'd not come back to the island for eighteen years, though she lived less than an hour away. Only work and wanting to prove herself to the rest of the team had compelled her to overcome the mental barriers that had kept her away. The island was where her best friend, Jodie, had been murdered, drowned in the lake, when Hannah was ten years old.

Her mind fogged, and her heartbeat thrummed in her ears. As if she was wearing headphones, all outside sound was muffled. She felt lightheaded as the sensation of floating overtook her.

She passed through the park entrance showing her badge to the woman in the kiosk.

Almost involuntarily, she found herself taking the turnoff that led to the remote stretch of beach where the murder had occurred. As the tires rolled over gravel, unclear images flashed at the corners of her mind. The memory of the sound of waves lapping on the shore made her breath catch. She was back at the place that had marked her life in a way that she could not overcome even after all these years. Only her sense of professionalism had eclipsed her fear about the past and the memories she'd locked into a dark closet. Maybe this was God telling her she needed to confront the event that had defined her life for so long.

Hannah pushed open the door and then let Captain out. He looked up at her with his teddy-bear face. She reached out to stroke his squarish, furry head. As always, it was a comfort to have her partner close. She was sure she saw empathy in his brown eyes. There was a reason the dogs in this breed were called gentle giants.

A chill September wind whipped around her when she made her way past a rocky outcropping and onto the white sand beach. As always, the lake had a faint rotten-egg smell. While she stood on the shore, she heard a boat in the distance.

For years she hadn't wanted to think about what had happened here. Only fragments of memory punctuated by black spots came into her mind. She wondered, too, if she had just adopted the newspaper accounts as her own memories because guilt and trauma made it impossible to recall the tragedy in any detail.

Jodie had gone out for a swim while Hannah had chosen to stay on shore to look for pretty rocks. Though she could remember the moments before the murder, she could not quite bring anything else into focus. The police told her that she must have seen the man who had drowned her friend. Yes, she had noticed a man approaching the beach, but she could not remember his face or what he was wearing. Had she turned away before he'd gotten close or was her mind blocking it out?

She shuddered as she walked closer to the water, shielding her eyes from the setting sun. Wind rippled her uniform. The boat that she'd heard earlier came into view, a small motorized craft with only one man in it.

Turning her attention back to the shore, she thought about the years of therapy to try to get past the tragedy and yet, it still held her prisoner. She'd even chosen to have a K-9 whose specialty was water rescue, thinking that she could prevent another child from suffering Jodie's fate.

Captain licked her hand, bringing her back to reality.

Time to get back to work. Convincing Trevor Gage he needed to accept the unit's offer of protection would be a challenge.

The man in the boat pulled it up on the beach and got out. He was far enough away that she could not see his face, but she recognized the park service uniform. He pulled a trash bag and poker stick from the boat and stabbed at a wrapper as he worked his way up the shore toward her.

Hannah turned sideways and watched the man when he leaned over to pick up a soda can. His baseball hat with the park logo on it partially shielded his face from view.

Why was her heart beating so fast?

The man kept working his way up the shore while she remained frozen in place. As he drew closer, he lifted his head and made eye contact.

A wave of terror engulfed her. She knew this man. The curly brown hair and close-set eyes. No, it couldn't be. Was this the man who had killed her friend? Her heart pounded when the long-buried image of a face escaped the cage she'd locked it in.

She took a step back. Maybe she was mistaken. It had been eighteen years. What were the chances he would come back to this spot? She shook her head as her heart raged against her rib cage.

The man continued to work his way up the shore. She couldn't look away. Was her mind playing tricks on her?

He must have sensed her staring. Now only fifteen feet from her, he looked right at her. His eyes grew wide.

As if to confirm her suspicions, a sort of brightness, like a light switch being thrown, came across the man's features.

Her stomach twisted.

He recognized her.

Even after all these years, Hannah's distinctive red hair would make her memorable.

The man tossed his bag and stick and darted toward her. With Captain close at her heels, Hannah turned to sprint back to her car, where she'd left her gun belt. The man closed in on her. She stumbled on the rocks, scraping her arm. Pain shot through her.

He grabbed the back of her jacket and yanked hard. The collar of her uniform dug into her neck.

Captain barked and leaped around them as they struggled.

Before she could cry out a command to her K-9, the man wrapped his arm around her neck and dragged her backward. The tight grip of his elbow cut off her breathing. Black dots filled her vision as she felt herself being dragged across the sand toward the water.

She tried to twist her body to break free. The man's other hand suctioned around her stomach. Hannah fought to remain conscious as it became harder to breath. Her vision was reduced to a pinhole. She managed to kick her assailant's shins. The move caused him to loosen his grip around her waist. Grabbing his forearm to pry it loose, she angled her body and twisted free. The momentum of her move propelled her forward, where she fell to the ground on all fours.

Captain's frantic barking pummeled her eardrums, as did the waves crashing against the shoreline. They were so close to the water's edge.

She pushed herself to her feet and turned to disable her attacker, landing a blow to his stomach. He groaned in response. A fist collided with the side of her head, disorienting her. He grabbed her hair, which had worked free of the bun she kept it in.

Water soaked through her shoes as he dragged her deeper into the lake. His hat had fallen off. She saw his face—just the flash of an image but crystal clear. The arched eyebrows and redness of his skin. His features were contorted into an expression of rage.

She clutched at his shirt. He pushed her into the water and was on top of her before she could react. As she flailed, his hand was full on her face, forcing her under.

Dear God, no, this can't be happening.

After all these years, she knew what Jodie's killer looked like, but she would not live to see justice.

The water enveloped her as she fought to stay conscious.

The noise of a barking dog caused Trevor Gage to draw his attention to the shore. Diverting from the trail where he'd been walking, he ran toward the lake. A large black wooly-looking dog paced the shore. He narrowed his eyes, trying to discern what he was seeing. The setting sun hitting the water made images murky. He saw the back of a man in a park employee uniform as he bent over in the waist-deep water. What had the dog so upset?

He drew closer, running past a patrol car with the Mountain Country K-9 insignia on it. He'd had more than one encounter with that multistate task force since the recent murders of men he had known when he lived in Elk Valley, Wyoming. The Mountain Country K-9 task force believed that he was the next target for the serial killer and that he should accept the unit's offer of a safe house. The loss of three of his friends ten years ago had been hard enough and now, it was starting all over again with three new victims.

The man in the water angled sideways.

Trevor's heart pounded when he saw a woman's head bob to the surface and then the man turned and pushed her under again. The woman thrashed in the water, her arms and legs flailing while the man held her down. The buoyancy of the salt water probably required extra effort to keep her head under, but she was still being drowned.

Still some distance away, Trevor broke into a run as he shouted, "Hey, you. Stop."

The man's head shot up. He glanced in Trevor's direction and then rushed toward a nearby boat, jumped in and yanked the rip cord. As the boat lurched forward, the man reached out and grabbed the floating woman, dragging her into deeper water.

Trevor slowed when he reached the rocky shore as terror surged through him. He hurried as fast as he could. His feet sank into the sandy beach, but he kept running.

It looked as though the woman had raised her head and shouted something.

The dog lunged into the water and swam toward the boat. The man in the uniform tried to push the woman back under from his position in the boat. As the dog drew closer, he let go of the woman and sped away.

The dog reached the woman and grabbed hold of her collar, then pulled her toward shallower water. Trevor ran into the lake up to his knees. Still holding the woman by her collar, the dog swam with a ferocious energy toward the shore.

The woman said something to the dog, who let go of her. She stood up in the waist-deep water, blinking and shaking her head.

Trevor stepped toward her through the water. "Are you all right?" he shouted. It seemed a ridiculous question to ask considering he had just witnessed an attempted drowning. The man in the park uniform was now a tiny dot in the distance. The engine noise had become a low-level hum almost drowned out by the waves hitting the shore. The culprit was long gone.

The redheaded woman caught sight of Trevor. Water dripped off her face and long hair. Her hand reached out for the back of the dog as they pushed through the water and got closer to him. Her slack jaw and wide unfocused eyes told him she was in shock. She shook her head in disbelief.

He hurried toward her.

When she drew close, he reached out and guided her to the shore, putting an arm across her back. "I gotcha." The dog followed dutifully beside her. Still supporting her, Trevor led her across the sand and up the rocky shore. She was dressed in a uniform with the MCK9 logo on the pocket and back of her gray jacket. The car he'd run past must be hers. No doubt, she had come here looking for him.

She gripped his arm. "I just need a moment." She sat down and stared at the ground. There was a cut on her arm.

"You're hurt. Can I look in your car for a first aid kit?"

She nodded without looking up.

He searched the car, finding a first aid kit under the front seat and a blanket. When he returned, the dog shook the water off his substantial fur coat far enough away not to spray her and then settled down beside the woman. Trevor wrapped the blanket around her, squeezing her shoulders before sitting beside her.

He flipped open the first aid kit. "Give me your arm. It's scraped up."

She twisted her arm toward her face. Her forehead furrowed as she examined the injury. "I fell on the rocks when he chased me." Her voice sounded faraway and disconnected. She was still in shock.

Cupping his hand under hers, he squeezed out some disinfectant from a tube, then placed a bandage over the cut and patted her forearm gently. "Better?"

Hannah drew the arm closer to her body, holding it at the wrist. "Thank you."

She stared at the ground. "I should call this in and make sure a report is filed. I need to catch the man who attacked me."

He wondered about the use of the word *I*, as if it was her sole responsibility to arrest the man who had tried to kill her.

"What happened out there? It looked like that guy was trying to drown you."

She nodded her head. "Yes, he was." She folded her arms over her chest and rocked. Her eyes glazed over.

"Who was he?"

"It's a long story." She lifted her head and stared off into the distance. Her response indicated it was not a story she was ready to share.

The dog pressed closer to her, making a sympathetic noise.

She clearly needed more time to recover from such a traumatic event. "Maybe you should take a second to catch your breath," he said.

She ran trembling fingers through her wet hair and let out a heavy breath. "First, I need to call this in." She rose to her feet. "I'm going to radio the park police. Maybe they can catch him. He works for the park. They might even know who he is."

With the dog trailing behind her, she walked to her vehicle. She opened the driver's side door, leaned in and retrieved the radio.

Trevor followed her. He listened as she gave the details of the attack, the kind of boat the man was in and what he looked like.

She put the radio back then looked directly at him for the first time. Light came into her eyes as recognition spread across her face. "You're Trevor Gage."

He nodded and then pointed toward the patrol vehicle. "I'm assuming you're here to talk me into going into a safe house since the phone calls didn't work." His tone was more defensive than he'd expected. The truth was the guilt he felt over his friends dying ten years ago—and all over again more recently—had never left him.

From the phone interviews he'd had with members of the unit, he knew they suspected that the murders might be connected to an incident he had been a part of ten years ago. All the victims, the first three and now three more recent ones, had been members of the Young Rancher's Club in Elk Valley. Trevor had asked a girl to a formal dance the club put on. He had really liked Naomi, but his friends had told her that she'd been invited as a joke. Maybe if he had been more forthright in coming to her defense none of the murders would have happened.

She crossed her arms. "I'm supposed to be protecting you, not the other way around."

"I'm just glad I showed up when I did," he said. "If I hadn't heard your dog barking, I wouldn't have known something was amiss."

The woman brushed her fingers over the dog's head. "We look out for each other."

The dog licked her hand.

"What's his name?"

"Captain." She held her hand out to him. "And I'm Officer Hannah Scott."

Hannah's grip was firm. The softness of her skin sent an electric pulse up his arm. Her hair must have been in a bun at some point, as part of it was secured and hanging off to the side. Even in her bedraggled state, she was a striking woman. Perhaps it was the green eyes. "You didn't call and say you were coming?"

"You stopped answering our calls. Besides, I

thought you would be more likely to agree to be taken in if you didn't have time to think about it."

He pressed is teeth together. "So that's the new tactic. An ambush from the Mountain Country K-9 team. I already said I could take care of myself."

"We're only trying to protect you, Trevor." Her words took on a biting quality that matched his tone of voice.

He shook his head but restrained himself from saying anything more.

He stared off toward the lake. He wasn't going to a safe house. Hadn't he made that clear?

When he turned in her direction, he noticed that her hand still trembled a little when she brought it up to her neck. Was she still upset from the attack or was this about his refusal to cooperate with her plans for him?

She was clearly shaken. He couldn't just leave her here.

"Why don't we drive back to my RV so you and I can get dried off? You can have a moment to catch your breath."

She turned in his direction. "Did you walk here?"

"Yes, I was out trying to clear my head." The truth was, he had been thinking about the RMK and what he could do to catch him. Trevor could handle himself, and he'd grown up shooting guns. Coming to the island had been partly to get away from the busyness of Salt Lake, but he wondered if his being in the open would draw out the killer and end this whole nightmare. From the questions he was asked in interviews, he'd deduced who the main suspects were. Even if the RMK was Ryan York and not Naomi Carr's brother, Evan, Trevor felt a responsibility for the killings. If he had called out the other young men on their behavior all those years ago, even if he'd never acted that way toward a young woman, maybe no one would be dead. "What do you say? Do you want to go back to the RV to get dried off?"

She glanced down at her soaked uniform. "I guess that's what we should do. Plus, you really shouldn't be out in the open by yourself."

After Hannah loaded her dog in the back of the vehicle, she got behind the wheel. He directed her to where his campsite was.

They drove past a herd of buffalo. The island was famous for its wildlife, including the antelope it was named for, as well as bighorn sheep, foxes and an abundance of birds. The land around them was flat but mountains were visible in the distance. When he glanced through the back window, the silvery lake had just slipped out of view.

"So that guy who came after you. Do you know who he was, or was it a random attack?"

She shook her head and stared through the windshield. "It's a long story." Her voice had taken on that flat disconnected quality again.

He longed to know the reason behind such a violent attack, but it was clear she wasn't ready to share. If the attempted murder was for personal reasons and hadn't been random, he wondered if the guy would come after Hannah again. Probably, if he wasn't caught soon.

The prediction the MCK9 unit had made was that he would be the RMK's next victim and that had been the plan from the beginning. That meant that both he and Hannah had targets on their backs.

TWO

Hannah tried to quell her irritation at herself as she drove toward where Trevor had indicated.

Things had really gotten off on the wrong foot. How was she going to convince him that it was in his best interest for the team to protect him when his first impression of her was that she couldn't even keep herself from being attacked?

Her clothes, still wet from the lake, felt like they weighed an extra ten pounds. Her skin itched from the saltiness of the water.

Hannah looked over at Trevor just as he leaned toward her and pointed. Their heads nearly banged into each other. His soft hair brushed her cheek. She sat up straighter as her heart fluttered at his proximity.

The photo in his file really didn't do him justice. The shaggy blond hair and clear green eyes made him a very handsome man.

"Oh, sorry," he said, settling back into his seat rubbing his head. "I was just going to point out that the RV is just around that bend behind that blue camper."

"Got it." Her mind reeled with everything that had happened. If she was going to do her job, she knew she had to put the attack on the back burner. Maybe the park police would catch the man who had tried to drown her—the man who had probably killed Jodie. The thought caused a chill to run down her spine.

"You okay?"

"Yes, fine." She wasn't sure what to think about Trevor. He'd shown a great deal of courage and compassion in rescuing her.

The RV, along with other tents and campers, came into view. The campsites were fairly far apart. The sky had turned a soft shade of pink as the sun hung low in the sky.

"Breathtaking view, isn't it?"

She nodded.

"It's worth it to come out here just for the sunsets." His voice filled with appreciation as he leaned closer to the windshield. "The night sky is something else, too, with so little artificial light to obstruct the view."

"Yes, I know. My family used to come out here all the time," she said. "I just don't think it's a good time for you to take a vacation. You're in more danger by being out here alone."

"Of course, I'm aware of the threat on my life. I've had several phone calls with your boss…

what's his name? Chase Rawlston." A defensive tone had invaded his words. "I'm also a grown man who can make his own decisions."

She let out a breath and glanced at the roof of the car. Tension settled around her like a lead blanket. As if things could not get worse. Out of the frying pan and into the fire. How was she going to get this whole mission back on track?

Convincing Trevor to accept protection was her first big assignment with the Mountain Country team. Although she'd done some training and helped out in Elk Valley last month, including interviewing Evan's ex-girlfriend, Paulina Potter, she still felt like she needed to prove herself.

Hannah pulled up to the RV, where a blue truck was parked. The logo for Trevor's ranch consulting business was on the driver's-side door.

Both of them stared out their side windows for a long moment.

"Look, I appreciate what you and your team are trying to do," said Trevor.

How could he be so obstinate? She met his gaze. Afraid of saying the wrong thing, she simply nodded. She worried that her coming out to convince him in person had set things back rather than moved them forward. She grabbed her gunbelt and pushed open the door. Once they both got out of the patrol car, she opened the back door and spoke to Captain. "Dismount." The dog lunged to the ground with an easy agility.

Trevor reached into his pocket and withdrew a key. He stared off into the distance. "I still can't get over that sunset." His voice softened.

She was drawn to a man who could appreciate sunsets and night skies. "How can you get any work done out here?"

"Most of my ranch consulting work is remote right now. I wouldn't want to put any of my clients in danger." He swung open the door and gestured that she could go ahead of him up the two metal stairs. Captain trailed behind her.

The inside of the RV, which looked to be over thirty feet long, was quite spacious, with a table, seating area and kitchen. He pointed toward a pocket door. "Bathroom is back that way. I'm sure you want to wash the saltwater off."

His comment made her itch her forearm. The lake had a higher salt content than the ocean.

"I can loan you one of my shirts and sweats while I get your uniform washed up."

"You have a washer and dryer in here?"

"No, not quite enough space for that. The campground has a community room with washers and dryers."

He opened the pocket door, revealing a queen-size bed and a door off to the side. He pulled out some clothes for her in the drawers beneath the bed. "The bathroom is behind that door."

She showered and changed quickly. When she stepped out into the main living area, Captain was sitting at Trevor's feet. The dog thumped his tail when he saw her.

She handed Trevor her wet clothes. He excused himself and headed out the door. Hannah took a seat at the table, where she could see him through the window as he walked with an easy gait toward a concrete building painted white.

Once he went inside the building, she stared around the small space. The signature silver Stetson he wore in the photo she'd seen rested on a hook. She rose to examine the books on a short shelf above the couch. A lot could be revealed about a person by what he read. And she was curious about who Trevor Gage was beyond what the file had told her.

There were several paperback westerns, a guidebook for Antelope Island, a book about prayer and one about apologetics that she'd read.

Trevor cleared his throat. She hadn't realized he was standing on the threshold of the RV.

Heat rose up in her cheeks. "Sorry, you caught me snooping."

Shrugging his shoulders, he took a step inside the RV. "I do the same thing when I'm at someone's house. You can learn a lot about a person by the books on their shelf."

"Exactly." She was a little stunned to hear her thoughts coming out of his mouth.

"And what would I find on your shelf if I got a chance to look?"

She liked that he was curious about who she was as a person. She pointed to his book on apologetics. "This. Some mysteries, a book about watercolor painting for beginners." She wanted to tell him that there was a whole section on her bookshelf about how repressed memories and recovery from trauma worked, but she held back that information, knowing that she didn't want to fall apart in front of him. She had been enough of a hot mess after the attack. If she was going to achieve her mission, she needed to repair the impression he had of her as a law-enforcement professional.

But the look in his dancing green eyes was so inviting, she wanted to share more.

He raised an eyebrow. "Watercolor painting?"

"I dabble. I'd like to take some classes someday."

He nodded and then stepped toward the kitchen counter. "Gonna be a while before your uniform is washed and dried. Can I get you something to drink, a soda or flavored water?"

"Water would be nice." She took a seat at the table.

He opened the tiny fridge, pulled out a plastic bottle and set in front of her. He grabbed a soda for himself and sat opposite her.

She took a sip of water and glanced out the window at the now dark sky. Was the man in the park uniform still out there searching for her? The thought made her shudder.

She'd come to visit Trevor with a goal in mind, but what could she say that wouldn't cause him to become defensive? It seemed he'd dug in his heels.

Trevor traced the water stain his soda can made on the table as a tense silence enveloped them.

Captain huffed and whined.

Her sentiments exactly. Her partner's verbal response captured the level of frustration she felt.

She was at an impasse as to what her next move should be. "You know, I think I better call my boss on the task force and let him know what happened."

"You can go in the other room if you want some privacy."

She moved to the end of the RV and closed the pocket door behind her before she dialed Chase Rawlston's number.

Chase picked up after two rings. "Hannah, good to hear from you. Any progress on getting Trevor Gage to take up our offer of a safe house?"

"Not really, and things have just gotten more complicated." After a deep breath, she relayed to him about being attacked and nearly drowning, explaining that she was pretty sure it was the same man who had killed her friend all those years ago.

"That sounds like a lot to go through. Are you okay?"

She sucked in a breath through her teeth. "I have to be okay, right? I have a job to do."

Chase did not answer right away. When he did, his response was slow and measured. "Do you think this man will come after you again?"

Her throat constricted and she squeezed the phone. "Yes. I think the only thing that protected me all these years is that I couldn't identify him. This is my first time back to the island since Jodie died. Seeing him and being on the island must have jarred the memory I had repressed because of the trauma."

"Sounds like you could use some protection yourself," he said.

"I need to see this thing to the end. I want this guy in prison for what he did to my friend. If I'm out in the open, he's more likely to make an appearance, and I'll be ready for him next time."

"All the same, the team will offer you some protection."

She didn't want to be the one who needed protecting. She wanted Chase to see she could do her job. "Trevor has some distrust toward the task force. I'm not sure why. I would like a little time alone to convince him to go into a safe house."

"Okay, you have a night. In the morning, part of the team will come over there to provide both you and Trevor with some protection."

"I appreciate that. There is a chance the RMK could follow Trevor here."

"The last sighting was in Salt Lake. We will assume he's still here until more evidence comes in. That's why some of the team will stay here." He paused. "Hannah, are you sure you don't want to take a sabbatical from the task force and the RMK case until the guy who came after you is brought in?"

She closed her eyes and pressed her lips together. This was the question she'd dreaded. Being part of the Mountain Country Task Force was a real feather in her cap, but not if she was sidelined. Plus, she had grown fond of the other members of the team and their K-9 partners. "I'm the only one based out of Salt Lake, so I think I should be the one to handle this. Besides, Trevor saw the guy, too. I think we can help each other." If Trevor would accept the help.

"If the guy is a park employee, it shouldn't take that long to track him down."

"That's what I was thinking. The park police already have a description of him. This could be over quickly for me, and I would hate to miss out on helping the team bring in the RMK."

"Maybe I can help persuade Trevor. Can you put him on speaker?"

"Sure." She pushed open the pocket door. Trevor was holding his soda and staring out the window. With the phone in her hand, she stretched out her arm after pushing the speaker button. "My boss wants to talk to you."

Trevor stepped toward her. The *W* that formed between his eyebrows and his narrowed eyes suggested he wasn't happy about being put on the spot to talk to Chase.

Choosing to ignore the shift in mood, she spoke into the phone. "He's here."

Trevor moved closer to the phone.

"Trevor, you understand the risk you're taking by choosing to remain out in the open." Chase adopted a neutral tone of voice.

"Yes, it's my decision," he said.

"I wonder if you would be open to accepting Officer Scott's protection at least for tonight."

"You mean like she's my bodyguard." He locked her into his gaze as his mouth formed a tight line, communicating disapproval. "I'll think about it."

Her heart sank. He wasn't showing much confidence in her abilities.

"Do that," said Chase. "Some of the team will be coming over there tomorrow early. We'll talk some more." He said goodbye to Hannah and disconnected.

They stood only a foot apart. Her eyes searched his. "Why are you doing this, Trevor? Putting yourself in danger? You're not a trained law-enforcement officer."

He turned away, running his hands through

his blond hair, then massaging the back of his neck. "What happened ten years ago wrecked me. Yes, my friends were immature, but why didn't I speak up with more force before it got out of hand?" His voice faltered. "And now, it's happening again, the murders of people I cared about. All because of me."

"We don't know for sure if it was because of the incident at the dance. All we know is that members of the YRC are being targeted. There are two suspects who have reason for going after the men who were in that club." Though they had interviewed Evan Carr early on, both he and Ryan York had fallen off the radar and been impossible to contact, making them both look suspicious. Plus, when she and Chase had interviewed Evan's ex, she'd finally confessed that she had lied about Evan being with her at the time of the murders. There was an unaccounted-for hour when he would have had time to shoot the first three victims.

"No matter who the killer is," Trevor said, "this is about the caliber of bad behavior that the members of the club fostered. I should have said something about the way they were treating women. I should've stopped it. I have to do something to make this right." His face contorted with anguish. He retreated to the table, where he'd left his soda. He took a long swig, then crushed the can in his hand and tossed it in a tiny trash can.

"I can appreciate how you feel." The emotion in his voice tore through her and caused a tightening in her own stomach. "You should let law enforcement take care of this though."

He turned to face her, shaking his head. "Really, it doesn't matter if it was about the dance or not. Yes, many of my friends in the club were immature, but that doesn't excuse their behavior. I wasn't a Christian back then. But common decency should have made me call the guys out on some of the things they chose to do."

"You can't undo the past." No one knew that better than she did.

"I get that. I thought I had forgiven myself for the self-absorbed way I was back then. But these new murders made me realize there is a whole other layer I have to deal with."

"Self-forgiveness is hard." She knew she was speaking about herself as much as him. She felt a level of responsibility for Jodie's death. Why hadn't she stayed closer to her friend?

"Tell me about it," he said.

She realized they were both choosing to make themselves bait for a killer to see that justice was done. "I think I understand. We have more in common than you realize."

What are you talking about?"

Taking breaths between phrases to calm her nerves, she relayed to him what had happened to Jodie all those years ago.

Trevor remained attentive and silent while she told the whole story of how her best friend had died. When her voice faltered or she choked up, she found warmth and caring in his eyes. "All these years I keep thinking that I could have prevented her death, or at least been more helpful in catching the killer."

"You were just a kid," he said. He rested his hand on her forearm. "That's a lot for a ten-year-old to deal with." His fingers warmed her skin as his voice filled with compassion.

His response to her story had been so gentle, she found her attitude toward him softening. She finished with a final comment. "I think that man we both saw is the one who killed Jodie. Why else would he attack me?"

He nodded. "That means you have a whole new set of complications to deal with. It's a lot for anyone to handle."

Though she was drawn to his kindness and the intense warmth she saw in his eyes, she caught herself, pulling back her head. She reminded herself that she was here to do a job. He already didn't think she was competent enough to protect him. Had opening up to him been a mistake? Best to keep this on a professional level.

He excused himself, saying that he would put her uniform in the dryer.

He returned a few minutes later. "Look, are you hungry? You might as well eat something while you wait for your clothes to dry." His voice had taken on a businesslike quality.

Did he think she was leaving after her uniform was washed?

She hadn't had time for dinner before she came out to the island. "Sure, that sounds nice."

He opened his dorm-size fridge. "Burgers all right?"

"That would be delicious. Can I help?"

"The cooking area is only big enough for one. Why don't you sit and relax?"

She took a seat at the table while Captain settled on the floor beside her. The burgers sizzled in the pan.

Trevor turned to face her. "This is getting real, isn't it?"

It wasn't fear she saw in his face. The hardness of his jawline and his steady gaze suggested resolve.

"It was never a game." She nodded, shaking off the fear that invaded her awareness. To protect Trevor and deal with the man who attacked her, she needed to remain clearheaded.

As he lifted the burgers from the pan and placed them on the buns he'd pulled out, Trevor wrestled with a sense of anticipation and fear. If he could help catch the RMK, there would be some justice for the friends he'd lost. If all this was because of what had happened with Naomi, he was the catalyst that had set this violence into motion. Hiding in the safe house was not the answer. Staying out in the open meant he could draw the killer out and end this once and for all.

He placed a jar of pickles, and bottles of ketchup and mustard on the table and then set a paper plate with the burger on it in front of Hannah. He took a seat on the other side of the table.

Captain raised his head and sniffed the air.

Despite his size, the dog seemed to have a sweet, mellow temperament.

Hannah reached down and ruffled Captain's head. "He does make people smile."

From where he sat, Trevor stretched his arm the short distance to the counter, opened a drawer and grabbed a fork, which he set on the table. "For the pickles," he said.

She grabbed the jar and put pickles on her burger. She looked at him with a piercing gaze. "I'm on guard duty for the night whether you like it or not until the rest of the team can get here."

The pleasantries of sharing a meal vaporized with her strong words.

Hannah had initially shown such a vulnerable demeanor, the force of her words took him by surprise. "Fair enough. I have a gun, too. I go to the range every week." Then again, his first encounter with her had been right after she'd nearly lost her life.

"Let me do my job," she said.

He nodded and squeezed some mustard onto his burger. Despite the attack, she seemed to be getting her spunk back. Maybe he was seeing the real Hannah now, assertive and direct.

They both ate their meal in silence. Like him, she was probably lost in her thoughts about the gravity of the situation.

Captain rose to his feet and licked his chops. As the minutes passed, two lines of drool formed on his jowls.

Trevor chuckled. "He's pretty convincing."

"Yeah, I know, you'd think he was starving to death, but I fed him earlier. He won't take food from you, though, even if you offered it. He's trained to only accept it from me."

"Why is that?"

"To prevent him being poisoned." She lifted the burger. "This is really good. Cooked to perfection."

Focusing on Captain seemed to make them more relaxed around each other.

"Thank you."

After the meal was cleaned up, Trevor moved toward the door. "Your uniform should be dry by now."

Hannah rose to her feet. "I'll go get it."

"There are only three washers in there. Your uniform is in the one on the south-facing wall."

She commanded Captain to follow her and stepped outside.

From the small window, he watched as she headed toward the laundry room. He could see light from a few other campsites. Though the weather was nice in the fall and there were fewer bugs, most of the campers came in the summer.

He studied the darkness beyond the campsites.

Hannah and Captain returned. After pulling the gun from her utility belt, she placed the belt on the counter. She put the gun on a shelf, within easy reach. She retreated into the bedroom and returned to the main area of the RV wearing her uniform. Her hair had been pulled back into a bun.

Trevor retrieved his laptop. "I need to get some work done." Focusing on his job might take his mind off the looming threat. He sat down on the couch.

"Don't let me bother you. I have a book on my phone I can read." Captain positioned himself by the door.

The minutes ticked by as Trevor only half paid attention to the emails he needed to send and the financial statements he looked over. He found himself sneaking looks at Hannah as she read her book.

When she glanced over at him, he turned away as heat rose in his cheeks. Trevor drew his attention to the big shaggy dog whose mouth was hanging open. "Glad you're watching out for me, buddy." He yawned and stretched. "Think I'll get some sleep. You're staying up, are you?"

"Yes. That is what guard duty entails." She raised her eyebrows. "Like I said before. That's the plan."

He wasn't about to argue with her.

He nodded. "Okey dokey."

He put his laptop away in a drawer. She settled in on the narrow couch. Trevor excused himself and retired to the sleeping area, closing the pocket door behind him. He pulled his own gun out of a drawer and set it under the unused pillow.

Sleep was slow in coming, but he eventually drifted off. Somewhere between dreaming and alertness, he heard a banging noise.

Startled, he sat up in the darkness. He had the sensation the RV had been shaken, but he couldn't discern if it was real or he had simply dreamed it.

"Hannah?"

When he heard no reply, he pulled back the covers and placed his feet on the floor. Grabbing his gun, he reached for the pocket door and slid it open.

His heart pounded. The door to the RV swung on its hinges. Both Hannah and Captain were gone.

THREE

Captain kept pace with Hannah as she raced through the campground. In the darkness, she could hear the man who had tried to break into Trevor's trailer, though she could not see him clearly. She followed the sound of pounding footsteps past several RVs and a tent.

The air around her fell silent. She stopped and listened, still gripping the gun she'd grabbed earlier. Her heart pulsed in her ears as Captain brushed against her leg. The air around her felt electrified.

She could see the outlines of several more RVs and campers, before the area opened up to flat desert-like brush. Only a few exterior lights above RV doors were on at this hour.

She turned slightly just as a force like a brick wall hit her. She fell to the ground on her back. Hands suctioned around her wrist, holding her in place. In the darkness, she could not see the face of the man who loomed above her. She could hear him gasping for breath.

He released one of her wrists. Fingers pressed on the sides of her throat. The collision had caused her to drop her gun. She reached a hand out for where she thought it had fallen, patting the dirt.

Captain barked and circled around her.

Giving up on the gun, she sought to free herself from the clutches of the attacker. With her free hand, she punched him hard on the side of the face. The man groaned in pain, but the blow only caused him to clamp his fingers tighter around her neck.

Struggling to breathe as black dots formed in her field of vision, she knew she had only moments before she passed out.

Captain's barking intensified. He moved in closer and growled.

"Go away," said the attacker.

The distraction Captain created caused the man to loosen his grip, and she managed to punch his solar plexus. The man gasped. Twisting her body so she was on her stomach, she crawled out from beneath him.

Before she could get to her feet, he grabbed her leg. She flipped over but only managed to kick at air as he dragged her across the dirt. Sharp pebbles pressed into her skin.

Captain moved in, lunging at the man.

The man cried out. "Outta here."

Captain growled in response.

Again, he reached for her neck. She thrashed back and forth and gripped the man's wrist, seeking to keep him from tightening his hold as she struggled to breathe.

A thudding noise caused the man to let go of her. Her assailant bolted to his feet. From the ground, she saw the silhouette of two men fighting—no doubt one was Trevor—and heard blows being landed. Both men grunted and cried out in pain.

One of the men broke free and sprinted away. She heard footsteps coming toward her.

"You all right?" The voice was Trevor's, though he was no more than shadow in the darkness.

She pushed herself to her feet. "We have to catch him." She bolted into a sprint, searching and listening for any sign of the man who'd attacked her.

With Trevor and Captain at her heels, she headed across the flat open country in the direction she thought her assailant had gone. Her feet pounded the hard earth until she was out of breath.

All three of them stopped. She could hear Trevor gasping for air.

"I think we lost him," he said between breaths.

She didn't want to give up so easily. She had not seen the man's face. Was this the man who had come after her at the lake, or had the RMK changed his MO to get to Trevor and needed her out of the way? The man was the same build as the one who'd attacked her.

Only the sound of a car starting up in the distance made her realize Trevor was right. She ran a short distance toward the noise seeing only the faint red glow of taillights far away. The assailant had gotten away. Her shoulders slumped.

Trevor patted her back. "Let's head back to the RV and notify the park police about what happened."

She fought off the sense of despair that dragged on her spirit. "What would we tell them? I didn't see his face. I don't know what he was driving." Despite the lack of information, she knew a report would still need to be filed. The park police might provide additional protection until the team could get here.

In less than half a day, a suspect had gotten away from her twice. The situation felt a little hopeless. And she worried that this made her look less than competent to Trevor. "I need to find my gun. I dropped it."

They trudged back toward the RV park until they came to the area where the fight had taken place. With so little light, they both bent over and walked around. If she'd had time to grab her phone, she could have used the flashlight on it.

Once again, Trevor had come to her rescue. She had to give credit where it was due. "Thanks for helping me out."

"I wouldn't have known where to go if it wasn't for Captain's barking," he said.

"He's a good partner. Always has my back." Her foot came up against a solid object. She bent down, touching cold metal. "I found it."

Walking side by side, they headed back toward the RV.

"Thanks for looking out for me and going after that guy," said Trevor.

"Just part of my job." She did not hear in Trevor's voice the condemnation she directed at herself. "I wish I'd gotten a look at his face. I may have been his target."

Once back at the RV, Hannah phoned the park police and offered the scant details about the attack.

She ended by saying, "It would be good if you ran a patrol through here." She gave him the number of the spot the RV was parked in.

"We can assist with that," said the officer.

"It might be worth it to dust for fingerprints as well," she said. "He must have touched the door handle."

"We can do that when we have some daylight. Do you think this is related to the earlier attack on you?"

"It could be. It also might be that a man I've been assigned to protect was the target this time." She glanced in Trevor's direction.

Trevor, who was sitting on the couch, cleared his throat.

She looked directly at him. His expression suggested distress or even irritation. She wasn't sure which. She feared her frustration over losing the suspect had made her overstep a boundary in saying she was protecting him when he hadn't agreed to that. Was he upset with her or at the situation?

She turned her attention back to the phone call. She said goodbye to the officer and disconnected.

Trevor rose to his feet. "I'm going to try to get some sleep."

She took two steps toward him. "I meant what I said about protecting you. The whole team will. But we need a level of cooperation from you."

He studied her for a long moment. "None of this would be happening if I had just been more assertive ten years ago. No one would be dead. I want to do everything I can to catch this guy and make it right. If that means being bait, then so be it."

She shuddered from the force of his words and the steely look in his eyes. "I understand about guilt, but you don't need to risk your own life."

"Maybe I do." His words were saturated with intense emotion. "Good night." He turned without saying anything more to her, disappearing behind the pocket door.

Hannah plopped down on the couch. Captain sat at her feet. She reached out to touch his soft fur, then stroked his head and neck while her thoughts reeled. The voices of Jodie's parents filled her mind. Though they had not come right out and blamed Hannah, they had implied that she should have been watching out for their daughter. They wanted to know why she and Jodie hadn't gone out swimming together.

The image of the anguished expression on Jodie's mom's face floated in her mind as the words the distraught woman said echoed in Hannah's brain. *Why can't you remember what happened more clearly? You were there.*

But now that she'd seen the man's face, she did remember. Yet, none of that would bring back Jodie.

Yes, she knew all about guilt.

Hannah stared out the window at the darkness. Would the attacker come back and try a second time? She shifted in her seat, knowing that she could not stay awake all night.

Within twenty minutes, she saw headlights of a vehicle. She stood up and stared through the blinds to see the park police vehicle roll by slowly. The tightness in her chest eased a little.

It was a comfort to her that if there was any noise outside, Captain would let her know. She needed to be ready for another attack, no matter what.

The next day, Trevor woke up as the sun slanted through the blinds of his sleeping quarters. He dressed, washed his face and combed his hair before sliding open the pocket door. The aroma of coffee greeted him, but Hannah was not in the RV.

He swung open the door to find her standing not far from the RV with a steaming mug while Captain sniffed around and did his business.

She turned toward him and smiled. "I hope you don't mind. I made coffee."

With her red hair and emerald-green eyes, she really was quite beautiful. The spray of freckles across her round cheeks added a girl-next-door quality to her appearance. If he'd met her under different circumstances, he might've acted on his attraction. "Thanks for making the coffee."

"I heard from Chase. They're on their way. We need to get an early start today."

His stomach clenched. The use of the word *we* upset him. She was assuming so much. Just like she had done last night when she'd told the other officer she was protecting him. After a night's sleep, he'd realized why he was so resistant toward the unit's offer of protection.

It was his lack of faith in what he thought the police could do. Law enforcement had let down Elk Valley ten years ago. A cloud still hung over the town. Like his family, so many people had been wrecked by the murders and the lack of closure that they moved away. His father had sold a prosperous ranch in Elk Valley.

On some level, Trevor felt like it was all up to him to see that justice prevailed.

He took a step toward her. "What are you talking about?"

She sipped her coffee before answering. "Chase has secured the team a place to stay at the Fielding Garr Ranch here on the southeast side of the island. There are no permanent residences on the island, but the bunkhouse has been turned into sleeping quarters for park employees when they have a big project, and there's a meeting room close by where we can set up temporary headquarters while we wait to see if the RMK shows up."

He was familiar with the ranch she was talking about. It had not been a working ranch since the 1980s and now was a living museum and site where tourists could picnic, hike or take horseback rides. "I'm glad you were able to find a place to stay, but that doesn't mean I'm coming with you."

If his point in staying out in the open was to lure the RMK out, he wasn't sure that would happen if he was surrounded by cops.

Her eye twitched in response to his assertion. "Please hear me out. Some of the team that came down here will stay on the island and the other officers will be in Salt Lake in case the RMK makes another appearance in the city. You'll have a lot of protection, not just me." Her expression filled with earnestness as she stepped toward him. "You can't actually think you can catch this guy all by yourself and not be killed?"

She had a point. He didn't need to be foolhardy. His default position seemed to be to oppose her. She brought out his stubborn nature.

His thoughts raced as he looked into her green eyes. Twice now, she'd almost met her death at the hands of an assailant. Perhaps *she* needed *his* protection. Not that he would tell her that. "All right, I'll go, but I'm taking my gun."

"Is it legal?"

"Of course it is," he said. "I even have a conceal carry permit."

He picked up on the note of challenge in her voice and the defensiveness in his response as they stood face-to-face.

"If that's the way it's got to be…for now, but leave the gun here until I can clear it with Chase."

"Look, I have never been one to sit on the sidelines. That is just not my style. I'll go with you under one condition—you have to allow me to help catch this guy."

She lifted her chin as the muscles around her mouth tightened. "That's the only way you will agree to accept our protection?"

He put his hands on his hips. "That's the only way."

She folded her arms across her chest. "I'll have to clear that with Chase too. Please, just come with me for now."

The note of vulnerability in her voice made him cave. "All right then, let me get us some breakfast before we go." He saw that she was just trying to do her job.

After Captain was done, they stepped inside to finish their coffee. Trevor prepared a quick breakfast of cold cereal for both of them.

Hannah consumed the last few spoons full of cereal. "I think you should leave your truck here and ride with me in my vehicle."

His first instinct was to protest. He didn't want to be stranded without his truck. Then again, he could protect her more easily if they were in the same vehicle. "Sure, I'm taking my laptop, so I can get some work done."

"No problem," she said.

While she stepped outside, he grabbed his laptop and his gun, which he slipped into the laptop case. If he was going to protect himself and Hannah, he would need it.

Within a few minutes, they were sitting in Hannah's vehicle with Captain loaded in his kennel in the back.

They drove on the road that led to the ranch from the north part of the island. At this early hour, not many other cars were on the two-lane road.

Hannah glanced in the rearview mirror. "Something wrong?"

"I just don't know why that other car is following us so closely," she said.

He glanced over his shoulder at a white compact car. He couldn't see the driver due to the angle of the sun and the visor being down.

The turn off for the ranch was up ahead but still out of view. Hannah pulled over and the white car rolled by.

"Guess he wasn't following us. Can't take any chances of leading someone to headquarters." She pulled back out onto the road and drove.

She hit the blinker and turned where a sign indicated the ranch was. Silos, a sheep-shearing shed and a white stucco house came into view. Hannah drove along a dirt road past a brick building, several outbuildings and a display of farm equipment that probably went back to before the invention of the car.

She seemed to know where she was going. Chase must have given her directions.

She drove a little farther, past a crumbling brick structure parking in front of a long narrow building with several doors. A tall muscular man with brown hair and wearing the same uniform as Hannah stood outside the building talking on his phone. A German shepherd sat erect not too far from him. The officer waved at Hannah.

Hannah got out of her vehicle at the same time that Trevor did. The other officer walked over to them.

"Trevor, this is Officer Ian Carpenter. He just joined the team in July."

Trevor shook the man's hand.

"And that's his partner, Lola." She pointed toward the German shepherd.

Ian turned toward Hannah. "Chase told me what happened to you…about the attack. For your sake and Trevor's, we'll make sure someone is standing guard around the sleeping quarters and our meeting room." He bent his head toward the dog, who had not moved. "Since Lola's trained to protect and catch suspects, you'll be in good hands."

"Why don't you show us around?" Hannah turned toward Trevor. "You can meet the rest of the team."

"Sure, let me show you where you'll be sleeping first," said Ian.

Trevor glanced back at the way they'd come. On the drive to the bunkhouse, he had noticed several barns. He knew from the newspaper accounts of the other murders that all of the other victims had been shot in barns.

Antelope Island had few options for the team to stay if they were to have a presence. The only other building was the visitors' center and the only other place for lodging were the campgrounds.

Still, as his gaze rested on one of the barns, he wondered if they were giving the RMK ample opportunity to repeat the pattern of the other murders.

FOUR

After being shown to her sleeping quarters, where she would be rooming with the task force's tech expert, Isla Jiminez, and a sheriff's deputy, Selena Smith, Hannah followed Ian and Trevor one door down to a room with two bunk beds.

"You'll be rooming with Rocco and me," said Ian. "And the K-9s, so lots of protection." There was one other door to the bunkhouse. Chase and his K-9 partner, Dash, must be occupying that room.

Hannah still had her overnight bag from her trip up to Elk Valley in her patrol car. She retrieved it and put it in her sleeping quarters.

She and Trevor were ushered to the meeting room, a short walk from the bunkhouse. The meeting room looked like it may have served as mess hall for the cowboys who had once occupied the bunkhouse, or maybe it had been used by the family that had owned the farm for social gatherings. It had a functional kitchen and a large seating area with several couches, a fireplace and a long dining table.

Isla pulled computer screens and laptops from a box, then arranged them on a large fold-out table. She glanced up from a keyboard. Petite features and long brown hair enhanced her welcoming smile. "Hannah, good to see you."

Hannah stepped toward her colleague and hugged her. "Isla, this is Trevor Gage."

Isla held out her hand to Trevor. "Pleased to meet you. You're in safe hands with Officer Scott."

Trevor's response was simply to nod and say, "Oh?" Not exactly the vote of confidence Isla had given her.

Isla picked up an electrical cord and plugged it into the back of one of the computer screens. "We'll all be working hard to take in the RMK before he can get to you."

"I'm sure Chase has a game plan if he does show up here," said Hannah.

After finding an outlet for the electrical cord, Isla returned to the table. She stared at one of the screens while she tapped the keyboard. "In the meantime, I am going to familiarize myself with the island and make contact with some key people."

Trevor wandered off with his laptop and found a spot on one of the couches.

Hannah came around the table and stood beside Isla, who had already pulled up several maps of the island.

"I heard about what happened to you yesterday." Isla touched her dark brown hair at the temple, face filled with concern. "Chase informed the team."

"The man who came after me was wearing a park uniform. I was wondering if you might be able to pull up all the employees who work in this area that match his age and description. We might be able to figure out who he is."

"Sure, I can do that as soon as I get set up." Isla pushed back her chair and stood up.

"I know the RMK case needs to be your priority," said Hannah.

Isla wrapped an arm around Hannah's back, squeezed her shoulder and pulled her close. "I'm a major multitasker, Hannah, so no worries. And I just wanted you to know, I appreciate your courage in choosing to stay on the case."

"I didn't want to let the team down. I feel like I can make a substantial contribution since I'm from Salt Lake and know the area." Isla had had her own share of similar turmoil. Someone was trying to sabotage her efforts at becoming a foster mom, and it had escalated to her house being set on fire last month.

The rest of the team members slowly filed into the room—Rocco Manelli and his chocolate Lab,

Cocoa, along with Selena Smith and her Malinois, Scout.

Chase entered and gathered the officers on one side of the room. Rocco and Selena took a seat on the couch, while Hannah and Ian remained standing. Isla rolled her office chair closer to the group.

Trevor closed his laptop and moved to a nearby chair, so he could hear the conversation.

Chase paced the floor with his hands behind his back. He was a tall man with brown curly hair cut close to his head. In her time working at HQ in Elk Valley, Hannah had found him to be reserved but a good leader, always concerned for the members of the team. Perhaps some of his quiet nature was due to the tragedy in his life. A supervisory special agent with the FBI, Chase had come back to Elk Valley from DC after his wife and child had died in a revenge bombing.

Chase stopped and addressed the other members of the team. "Hannah informed me that someone tried to break into Trevor's RV last night. But the intruder may have been the man who came after Hannah when she got to the island. You all have been briefed on what happened to her at the lake."

Everyone nodded.

Hannah felt her cheeks flush. It was humbling to have become the victim of a crime instead of the one catching the law breaker. "I didn't intend to complicate this case."

"Could have happened to any of us," said Rocco. The rest of the team mumbled in agreement.

"We got your back," Selena insisted.

The show of support made her lower lip quiver. What a privilege that she'd been chosen to work with such a great group of officers.

Chase squared his shoulders. "Now for the big news. As you know the park police and employees have been informed about the RMK case. For now, we're not informing the public. We don't believe he's a threat to anyone but YRC members and we don't want to scare him off." Chase let out a heavy breath. "I just got a call. A man matching the description of the RMK was spotted walking a dog that looks like Cowgirl along the shore of the lake."

A tense hush settled in the room.

Hannah heartbeat revved up a notch. "So he's here on the island, and he still has Cowgirl."

Cowgirl was MCK9's missing therapy dog. Seemingly as a way of taunting the team's attempts to catch him, the killer had kidnapped the Labradoodle. She'd been brought in as a compassion K-9 for the residents of Elk Valley who'd been wrecked all over again by the recent killings. Cowgirl had been in the RMK's care for months now and was believed to have gotten pregnant. By now, she would have given birth. She had a distinct dark splotch on her right ear, making the RMK easy to spot when he was out in public with her. Despite sightings of a tall blond man with the dog in Idaho months back and the recent one in Salt Lake City, he'd so far evaded police.

Chase continued. "What we don't know is if the RMK is staying on this island or returning to Salt Lake. Some of the team members are still in Salt Lake, questioning witnesses and being ready in case there is another sighting reported. It's also possible the RMK could be staying in Syracuse, the town closest to the island. Lodging is limited here on the island, but he could be staked out in one of the campgrounds. Since it's clear he knows Trevor is here, this island is where we are most likely to catch him. Our job today will be to conduct a search of the island to see if anyone has spotted our man."

"We still don't know what he's driving?" Rocco asked.

Chase shook his head. "It's possible he would have changed vehicles by now, anyway, or even rented an RV."

Isla folded her arms over her chest. "I can call the RV rental places in the area and see if anyone matching the RMK's description made an appearance. He may have had Cowgirl with him, so he'll be memorable. The team members in Salt Lake can visit the RV rental places there. Sometimes you get better results with an in-person interview."

"Those puppies must have been born by now. I wonder where he's keeping them," said Selena as she played with a strand of her red hair.

"*If* he's keeping them." Ian's voice had become solemn.

So far, it appeared that the RMK had taken good care of Cowgirl. The hope was that he would do the same for her puppies.

Chase looked around the room. "We'll send people out in teams to cover the island. Isla, do you have a feel for the most efficient way to divide up the island?"

She swung back around to her computers and walked her rolling chair toward the table. "I got a basic feel for the area. The north end has more visitors with more amenities, so we should send one team up there and maybe have the other two teams deal with the middle and south side of the island, which is less populated but more area to cover."

Chase looked at Hannah. "Someone will have to stay here and keep guard over Trevor."

Trevor rose to his feet. "Actually, I'd like to go out and help catch this guy."

Hannah's stomach tied into a knot. She stepped toward Chase and whispered, "I meant to tell you. He agreed to come with me only if he could help out."

Chase placed a hand on her shoulder, leaning close to her ear. "We'll have to talk later."

Hannah gritted her teeth. She did not fail to pick up on the irritation in Chase's voice. This was her own fault for not communicating with Chase sooner and for not running Trevor's idea by him first. She had just so wanted to accomplish the mission she'd been sent on to show Chase she was worthy of her appointment on the team. She'd gotten tunnel vision about getting Trevor to agree to a level of protection.

Chase turned back to the whole group. "All right then—Trevor and Hannah will take the north side of the island. Rocco and Selena, you can handle the area south of the ranch. Ian and I will go to the place along the lake where he was last seen."

Isla sat back down at her computers. "I'm going to send each of you a map specific to the area that needs to be covered."

Chase nodded. "Be in touch via radio. Check in on a regular basis even if you don't have any news."

Trevor stepped forward. "I brought a gun with me. I train regularly."

"No." Chase glanced in Hannah's direction. "I can't allow that. Too much liability."

Hannah had not realized Trevor had brought the gun with him after she asked him not to. One more way he wasn't being forthright with her.

The team loaded their respective K-9s and headed out. Trevor got into the passenger seat of Hannah's vehicle.

As she sat behind the wheel, she could not hide her frustration with the situation. It came out in her tone of voice. "You ready to go?"

"Sorry, I didn't mean to get you in trouble."

She shook her head and turned the key in the ignition. "Let's just get to work." After checking the directions on her phone and looking at the map Isla had sent her, she pulled out of her parking space and headed toward the ranch exit. The first stop would be the visitors' center.

Trevor had ruffled her feathers. As she drove, she prayed for a sense of peace to return. The road stretched before her, with a view of the lake and the mountains beyond. She felt herself calming down. "Look, this whole thing has been a little sideways from the beginning. I didn't count on that man coming after me. The attack didn't allow me to present myself in the most professional way possible. Guess I made a bad first impression."

"Maybe you're looking at this wrong, Hannah?"

He hadn't said anything about his first impression of her. "What do you mean?"

"We can protect each other. Are you open to that?"

Though she did think they could help each

other, something in his suggestion pricked her insecurity about how he saw her as a police officer. "I can't put you in harm's way. It goes against my mission as a law-enforcement officer."

"It's a choice I'm making." He leaned toward her. "I told you why. I could say the same about you."

"What are you talking about?"

"Given what happened, wouldn't you be more secure if you went off duty and into a safe house? Or maybe you feel like I do—that making yourself bait might bring some justice to the situation."

She had to hand it to him—Trevor was perceptive. "That thought had occurred to me."

"Well then." He settled back down into his seat. "That's something we have in common."

The hard edges around their relationship seemed to soften a bit. She flexed her hands on the steering wheel. "I don't want my life to be defined by what happened when I was ten. But I feel like it is."

"I get that. I feel the same way about what happened in Elk Valley when I was eighteen. It seems to govern so many of the choices I've made in my life."

She glanced at him, appreciating the warmth of his expression, before she put her eyes back on the road.

She shook off the intense feelings. Just because

they had found a point of connection didn't mean they'd be picking out a china pattern together. She wasn't even sure what had made her think of such a thing.

"You still need to let me do my job," she said.

"I'm sorry I made you look bad in front of your boss," he said.

She drove on in silence, feeling the tight knot in her stomach return. She'd have to explain her choices to Chase and smooth things over. "I should've run the plan by him first. It is what it is."

Hannah turned into the visitors' center passing a large metal sculpture of a buffalo on the driveway leading to the parking lot. Once they found a spot, she unloaded Captain, and they headed toward a concrete building.

People milled around inside, looking at the displays about the wildlife and terrain. She spotted a ranger, an older man with a paunch, coming out of the gift shop.

The sight of the uniform caused a shiver to run down her back. The trauma of the attack was still with her. As if sensing the emotional shift, Captain leaned against her, his furry head brushing the back of her hand.

Trevor drew closer to her, as well. "You doing okay?"

Great, she was surrounded by empaths. It would be hard to hide any of her feelings.

She cleared her throat. "I'm thinking about asking that ranger if he knows who the guy is who came after me yesterday." She'd been so focused on today's assignment to look for the RMK that she hadn't stayed to talk to Isla about info she might have found out about her attacker.

The ranger offered her an inviting smile. She took a deep breath and moved toward him, hoping to get some answers on both of the cases.

Trevor stood beside Hannah as she got the ranger's attention. He was acutely aware of the people milling around him. Captain, in his K-9 vest, drew people's attention, but Trevor was tuned into anyone whose stare might be more menacing. To be out in the open like this was a risk, but he knew himself well enough that choosing to go into hiding would have been even harder. He had always been someone who made things happen, not a man who watched life pass by and let others do the work.

When the ranger turned toward her, Hannah spoke up. "Excuse me, I'm wondering if you have seen a tall blond man with a Labradoodle. The dog has a distinctive dark brown splotch on her right ear and the man usually wears sunglasses and a hat."

Trevor wondered if the RMK had a safe cool place to keep Cowgirl and the puppies. Having the dog with him would make the killer that much easier to spot. Certainly, he wouldn't come after Trevor with the dog in tow. He caught a flash of the brown uniform the rangers wore out of the corner of his eye. He whirled around and took a few steps toward the ranger, thinking it might be the park employee who had come after Hannah. Though he saw the ranger from the back, it was clearly a woman headed outside. He moved back toward Hannah. It wasn't just the RMK they needed to be worried about.

The ranger rested his hand on his paunch. "You must be with the Mountain Country K-9 unit. I saw the BOLO go out for that guy, but I'm not the one who called it in when he was spotted. Maybe he will make another appearance."

"That's what we're hoping for, so we can take him in," said Hannah.

"If he does show up, I'm sure we'll help you out as much as we can."

"We appreciate that." Hannah remained close to the ranger as her hand reached out to brush over Captain's head.

Her lingering indicated that she wanted to say something more but was hesitant. Her shoulders slumped. Trevor was pretty sure he knew what she wanted to ask. The trauma of the attempt on her life was probably still so fresh it was hard to talk about it.

He cleared his throat, hoping that he wasn't stepping out of line. "This officer is the one who was attacked by a park employee yesterday down by the lake."

Hannah gave him a sideways glance and an appreciative smile.

"I saw that report as well." The ranger turned toward Hannah. "I didn't realize it was you."

With a quick glance at Trevor, Hannah squared her shoulders, seeming to recover. "Do you have any idea who it might be?"

The ranger shook his head and ran his hands through his thinning hair. "The problem is the description is pretty generic. Average height. Curly brown hair."

"I get that." Disappointment permeated Hannah's voice. "It just seems like he would be easy to track down if he works for the park service."

"I don't even know how many rangers are employed around the lake—quite a few. And we got seasonal workers, as well. I can tell you that no one was assigned to pick up trash in the area where the incident happened."

"That's interesting," she said. "Why would he have been over there then?"

The ranger shrugged. "It could be that he had some downtime and decided to use it to clean up. Most park employees take a lot of pride in keeping the park nice and not allowing littering."

Hannah thanked the ranger just before a mom and her young daughter came up to the ranger to ask him a question. The man turned his attention to the woman and her child.

Hannah looked at Trevor. "Thank you for asking the question about the attack on me."

"I hope I wasn't stepping on any toes. It made sense to try and get that information from someone who might know."

"No, I appreciate it. Tracking that guy down might be harder than I thought it would be," she said. "There was nothing distinct about him that I remember. No scars or tattoos."

"Still, if he works for the park service, that narrows it down quite a bit. He's got to know you can identify him. Do you suppose he might take sick days and lay low so he doesn't get caught?"

Hannah's hand fluttered to her neck. "Honestly, I think he'd want to get rid of me before I could attach a name to him and track him down. Maybe he's already taken the uniform off, so he blends in more. Even if he does call in sick, I don't think he'll leave the island until… I'm dead."

Her voice trembled with fear. He found himself wanting to take her in his arms and comfort her. Instead, he bumped his shoulder against hers. "We'll catch him. Just let me know what I can do to help."

"Maybe Isla has pulled up employment files and will find a match. Now that my memory has been jarred, if I saw a picture of him, I would recognize him."

"What do we do next?" Trevor asked.

"We need to focus on finding the RMK. We should probably check all around this area inside and out. This is one of the busier parts of the island. Maybe we'll run into other rangers who might have seen him."

"We can split up and cover more ground faster." He angled away from her.

She grabbed his sleeve. "No, you stay close to me. That's the deal, right?" The look of insistence on her face reminded him of how quickly the tension could return to their relationship.

His intent had not been to antagonize her, but to try to be helpful. Why couldn't she see that? "Sorry, I didn't mean to step out of line. I know you're watching out for me."

"It's okay." Her voice softened.

With Captain by Hannah's side, they walked through the visitors' center and around the perimeter of the building, stopping at a birdhouse that was actually shaped like a Victorian house, with a tower-like structure on one end. Birds flitted around it.

He was struck by the view of the lake. There did not appear to be a single ripple and the mountains reflected perfectly in the water. The breeze rustled Hannah's red hair where it had slipped out of the bun. The soft wisps danced in the wind.

The air smelled salty. He relished the moment of calm and quiet. It was the reason he liked coming out here.

Hannah looked off in the distance. "I came here all the time as a kid with my mom and dad."

"Good memories?"

"They are all marred by what happened." She rested her hand over her face, covering her eyes. Captain sat at her feet and gazed up at her.

It was the most vulnerable he'd seen her since the attack.

She carried such a heavy burden. He placed a hand on her arm above her elbow. Though she did not pull away, she stiffened at his touch. After dropping her hand away from her face and raising her head, she swiped at her eyes and lifted her chin a little higher.

He pulled his hand away. Hannah seemed to be doing battle between processing what had happened to her and trying to come across as strong. Her defenses had gone back up.

What could he say to break through the armor she seemed to think she needed to have around him? "I know this is hard."

"Everything has just gotten so stirred up inside of me by coming back here, but I think it's for a reason. God wants me to deal with this once and for all. Seeing that Jodie's killer goes to jail will help, but it's also about healing my mind and heart, getting beyond what happened."

What she said applied to him, as well. Feeling the softness of the breeze over his skin, he understood that silence was the better response to the struggle she was going through. He was coming to admire her. There was something endearing about the fortitude and tenacity of her character.

Seeming to break the power of the moment, Hannah slapped her thigh. "I'm hungry. That cereal didn't stay with me. Why don't we go get something to eat after we check out the area around Bridger Bay? I think I saw a sign for a food place around that area. Stopping for lunch will give us a chance to question workers who may have seen the RMK."

They returned to the parking lot. As they walked through the lot, he noticed the white compact car that had followed them on the road before they got to the ranch.

Once they were settled in the car, Hannah pulled a notebook from her belt. "I saw that white car, too." She spoke as she wrote. "I made note of the license plate. Isla can run it. It could be that the driver is just a tourist going to all the touristy spots on the island."

"Yes, could be. That's amazing, though."

"What?" She shoved the key in the ignition.

"You memorized that license-plate number with a single glance."

She shook her head and shrugged. "It's a skill you gain as a highway patrol officer." Before shifting gears, she rested her gaze on him. "But thank you for noticing."

The warmth of her response did not go unnoticed. They were both making an effort to create a workable professional relationship for the time that they had to be together.

She pulled out of the lot. Trevor gave a backward glance toward the white car, which was parked away from the other cars. No one was moving toward it.

In any case, it was a reminder that they needed to be on guard.

FIVE

As she drove toward their next destination, Bridger Bay, where there was a much-used beach and a campground, Hannah took note of the vehicle some distance behind them. It first appeared as a shimmering piece of metal in the distance.

Like much of the island, the area where Hannah drove was flat, surrounded by desert-like vegetation, lots of sagebrush and prairie grass. She had a view of the mountains off in the distance. The flat terrain and straight road provided visibility for a long way. As the car drew nearer, she saw that it was a Jeep, dark green in color.

Though the island was not bustling with activity, they had encountered several other cars on this stretch of road. The car zoomed toward them as if to pass. Hannah slowed and veered toward the edge of the road to allow the other vehicle room to get around them.

Instead, the car rammed her bumper. Her body was propelled forward and then snapped back by the seat belt. Her jaw clenched as she gripped the wheel.

Trevor put his hand out, bracing it against the dashboard. "What's going on?"

He barely had time to finish his sentence before a second, more intense ramming caused the SUV to veer off the road. They bumped along over grass and rocks. When she checked the mirror, the car was still coming after them.

Captain made a noise of distress from his kennel.

Hannah pressed the accelerator, seeking to avoid another collision as she aimed the steering wheel back toward the road. This time, the other car scraped the passenger side of her SUV.

She twisted the wheel to avoid full impact. Trevor groaned. Still accelerating, she swerved in a wide arc. Her back end fishtailed as she went off the road on the other side. She cranked the wheel toward the road.

An oncoming car honked its horn as it narrowly missed her when she sought to get on her side of the two-lane road. The green car was still behind them.

Heart pounding, she pressed the accelerator to the floor. Another car came up behind the green Jeep and several more moved toward them in the other lane. Traffic was increasing as they got closer to Bridger Bay.

Even though the green car hung back, allowing another car to get between them, her heart still raced. When she checked the mirror, the Jeep was no longer visible. He must have turned off. Maybe the driver realized he'd be caught if he continued to follow them.

After catching her breath, she glanced at Trevor. "You okay?"

He massaged the back of his neck. "I'll survive."

"Did you get a look at the driver?"

He shook his head. "Everything happened so fast. Do you think it was the RMK?"

Her heart had still not slowed down. "Not really his MO. But it's possible he's getting desperate."

"Well, if it wasn't him, I'll give you one guess as to who else it could be."

She waited for her hand to stop shaking before reaching for the radio.

"This is Officer Hannah Scott. We just had an incident close to Bridger Bay. A green Jeep attempted to run us off the road."

Chase's steady voice came across the line. "Are you okay?"

"The SUV is a little dented up. We both might have a few bruises but otherwise okay."

"License-plate number?"

"No, I can tell you he's not following us anymore. He must have taken one of the roads or scenic turn offs before Bridger Bay," Hannah responded.

"Ian and I will go over there and have a look around. Rocco and Selena are farther south."

"Thank you," she said.

"I don't suppose you got a look at the driver?" said Chase.

"Neither one of us did."

"Now, after this, I'm not totally on board about you two being out in the open like that."

She was afraid he would say that. "We don't have enough personnel for me to be sidelined."

Chase did not answer. Static came over the radio.

"We're out here already. We can cover Bridger Bay and the nearby campsite. I don't know that we would be any safer at that ranch. Lot of people there, too."

Chase didn't respond immediately. "Point taken. We just don't have any other choice if we're going to stay on the island."

"My turn is coming up." The sign for Bridger Beach flashed by her on the side of the road. "Over and out." Best to disconnect before Chase changed his mind. She hit her blinker and turned off.

She found a parking space that looked out on the long stretch of beach and the Great Salt Lake beyond. She pressed her head against the headrest, closed her eyes and thanked God for His protection.

Trevor's warm hand rested on hers. "That was some stellar driving back there."

His touch sent warmth through her. She pulled her hand away even as her insides melted. "All part of my training." It made her feel good that she'd impressed him, but she needed to keep things professional.

Bridger Beach was one of the most popular spots for people to try floating in the Great Salt Lake. This late in the year, more people were probably just enjoying walking on the white sand. Taking Captain with them, they got out and walked the beach, stopping to talk to several people, but none of them had seen anyone matching the RMKs description.

The wind whipped around them and the air smelled of salt as she scanned the area. It was probably not worth their time to wait for the people who were swimming to come in.

Trevor turned toward her. "What now?"

"The campground is not too far from here. Maybe we should drive through it and stop to talk to a few people. The RMK might be staying there. For sure, people would remember Cowgirl."

"Okay," he said.

Tents, RVs, campers and three cottages populated the campground. Each of the far-apart spots had a gazebo. Hannah drove slowly, knowing that spotting Cowgirl would be the most likely give-away for their suspect. He might be taking the puppies out, as well, if he hadn't sold them. So far, the RMK seemed to be taking care of Cowgirl. She hoped the same was true for the puppies.

It seemed the RMK liked being spotted with the dog as a way of taunting the team. That's probably what his morning appearance was about—it was meant to instill frustration in the task force. Showing up on the island in such a public place was probably also intended to cause fear in Trevor. But to always have the dog in tow, and now, some puppies, would hinder the killer and make it that much harder to move stealthily toward his next intended victim. If he was staying on the island, it would have to be a camper or RV, not a tent—someplace the dogs would be safe if he left them.

She had to believe that searching the campgrounds was not futile. The door-to-door searches in police work could feel that way, and yet in her experience, being methodical usually turned up a lead.

They stopped at several campsites where people were outside cooking on the firepit or relaxing beneath a canopy. No one at the first two sites had noticed a man with a Labradoodle.

They stopped at a third site on the edge of the campground. An older couple sat beneath the gazebo in lawn chairs. Their truck camper was parked off to the side. The man rose from his seat as Hannah approached. Trevor followed behind her.

The man pointed at her SUV. "K-9 unit, huh?"

"Yes," she said.

"I used to train bloodhounds for the sheriff's department down in South Carolina. What kind of dog do you work with?"

Hannah perked up a bit. That meant the man was probably retired law enforcement. He'd be more likely to share info with her, and he probably was more observant than the average person. "A Newfoundland." She turned slightly toward the vehicle, where Captain was still secured in the back seat. "He's a good partner and a big ol' sweetheart."

The man took off his baseball hat and rubbed his thinning white hair. He studied Trevor for a long moment, probably wondering what his role was if Hannah already had a partner and why he wasn't in uniform.

"Trevor is assisting me in my investigation," she said. There was no need to share more details.

The man lifted his chin and nodded as if the explanation seemed to satisfy him. "Saw you driving through the campground. Looking for someone?"

Hannah nodded. "A tall blond man, usually wears sunglasses and a hat. He might have had a female Labradoodle with him who recently gave birth. The dog has a dark splotch on her ear."

The woman who had been sitting in the chair fanning herself piped up. "I saw a man matching that description yesterday evening."

"Here at this campground?" That meant that he must have stayed in the park last night before making his early morning appearance.

"Yes, I was taking Mr. Baby out for his evening constitutional." The older woman pointed at a basket by her chair that Hannah hadn't noticed before. A fluffy ball of brown-and-black fur was curled into a *C* shape.

Trevor stepped forward. "Where were you at when you saw the man?"

The woman pointed off in the distance. "There's a walking trail not too far from here."

Hannah's heart skipped a beat. This was the break they had been looking for. "Did you talk to the man at all?"

"Only briefly. His dog came up to me and was just so friendly. Our conversation was mostly about how cute the dog was."

Hannah piped up. "I don't suppose you saw his campsite or what he was driving?"

"We weren't close enough to the campsites for me to see which pad was his, and he didn't mention where he was staying or what he was staying in. The one thing I did notice about the dog was that it was clear she must be nursing puppies. Her teats were swollen, and her belly was stretched out as though she'd given birth recently."

"Thank you. You've both been very helpful."

"Mind if I meet your partner?" The husband's voice had a hopeful lilt to it, as if he was probably recalling his days of having worked with K-9s.

"Sure." Normally, she wouldn't have allowed someone to pet Captain while on duty, but the man seemed so overjoyed, and he and his wife had given her a break in the case. Plus, she could use an ally and a pair of eyes in the camp if the RMK was still here.

She opened the back car door and tripped the release on the kennel. Captain stuck his big furry head out so the man could pet him.

"What is his training specialty?" The man put his head close to Captain's.

"Search and rescue, mainly water."

After sweet talking to Captain for a moment and sharing a story about a dog he'd trained to search swamps, the older man thanked Hannah.

"Both the wife and I will keep an eye out for the man you're looking for."

Hannah handed him her card. "Call this number if you notice anything."

Despite her growling stomach, Hannah felt a sense of elation as she and Trevor both climbed into the SUV.

She radioed Chase with the news, ending by saying that they should maybe set up a stakeout of the campground. "I know he might be moving from campground to campground, but it's worth a try. He may still be staying here. Someone is bound to notice or hear the puppies sooner or later."

"Yes, that makes sense," said Chase. "There are several campgrounds on the island, but it seems like a good strategy to focus on the place we know he stayed at."

She gripped the radio a little tighter. "Any sign of the green Jeep?"

"Negative. We searched the area where you thought he must have turned off and questioned a few people, but we didn't come up with anything. Hannah?"

"Okay, thanks." Her voice wilted from disappointment.

"I think you and Trevor should come back to the ranch for now, given what happened with that Jeep."

"Am I going to be part of the stakeout?"

"Meadow is one of the officers who stayed behind in Salt Lake in case there was another sighting there. Now that we know the RMK is staying on the island, it makes sense to have her help us out. The remaining members of the task force will stay in the city in case the RMK returns there."

"What are you saying?"

"I think the safest thing for both you and

Trevor would be to come back to the ranch. With an extra officer, we should be able to proceed with the search. Meadow's K-9 has tracking skills, which will be a help."

Not what she wanted to hear. "Okay, we're going to pick up some food and then we'll head over there." She knew better than to argue with Chase. She already wasn't on his good side.

"See you in a bit," said Chase. "And, Hannah, you did good work today. I'm sure that car chase left you rattled, and you did your job, anyway."

"Thank you." Hannah clicked off the radio. The sense of elation she felt at having gotten a lead about the RMK eased the pain of knowing that she probably wouldn't be part of the stakeout.

The decision had been made. She needed to abide by what Chase wanted.

Trevor had heard the conversation. "Tough break. You don't like to be on the sidelines any more than I do."

She smiled. One more thing they had in common. "I just don't know if we will be any safer at the ranch."

It could be that the RMK had already figured out the team had set up headquarters at the ranch. The bunkhouse was separated from some of the busier parts of the ranch, but the patrol vehicles would give them away. If the RMK had figured out where they were staying, it would just be a matter of time before he came after Trevor.

* * *

Trevor's heart went out to Hannah. She seemed to shrink in the driver's seat. Her features were less animated. The look on her face was pensive. He liked the exuberant Hannah he'd seen moments before, when her solid police work had moved the investigation forward.

"It wasn't safety that I signed up for when I made my decision to stay out in the open," said Trevor.

"Me, either." She turned the key in the ignition.

"If you weren't such a good police officer, so interested in justice, you would have hung up your gun and headed to a safe house yourself," said Trevor.

"True." She rolled through the campground and back onto the road. Within minutes, signs for the Island Buffalo Grill came up. It was short drive before they entered the parking lot, where several other cars were parked. As long as the fall weather remained nice, people still visited the island. This was his favorite time of year to be here—less heat and fewer bugs.

Trevor noted that there was no drive-through, which would have left them less exposed.

Hannah turned off the car. "As long as we're here, it won't hurt to ask the kitchen staff if they have seen the RMK or know the park employee who tried to kill me."

They stepped inside, where only two other

people waited in line to give their orders. After Hannah ordered a cheeseburger and fries and paid, she asked the female clerk if she'd seen a tall blond man with a Labradoodle or puppies, and then described the park employee who had come after her. The clerk thought for a moment and then said, "No, I can't say that I have seen either of those men."

Trevor stepped forward and ordered a bison burger and onion rings.

While they waited for their food, they sat down at a table. Hannah stood up when she noticed a man wiping down a nearby table. She walked over and preceded to talk to him. The man shook his head. Once their meals came in to-go boxes, they headed out to the K-9 vehicle.

Hannah set her box on the console between the seats while Trevor dug into his onion rings. She took a couple bites of her burger and ate a hand-ful of fries before starting the car and heading back toward the ranch.

They sped past one of the scenic turnouts. He thought he saw something in his peripheral vision. Trevor craned his neck to get a look through the rearview mirror. "The green Jeep is back there."

SIX

After making sure there were no other cars close, Hannah spun the SUV around and pressed the accelerator. She could see the Jeep up ahead as it pulled onto the road.

The needle edged past seventy as she sought to close the distance between herself and the other car. She grabbed her radio and pressed the talk button. "Be advised. We are in pursuit of the green Jeep headed north from the Island Buffalo Grill. I could use some backup."

Chase's voice came across the line. "Headed in that direction. We're still in the area." Chase disconnected.

Her heart pounded as she kept her eyes on the road, passing the one car between her and the Jeep. The Jeep maintained speed as it turned off on a spur road that indicated it led to a trailhead.

She took the turn so tightly and at such a high speed that the tires spit up gravel that sprayed against the side of her vehicle. They headed up a twisty road, eventually coming to a dirt parking lot where only one other car was parked by a trailhead marker. The Jeep continued beyond the parking lot over the rough terrain. Hannah followed as both cars climbed a hill. The Jeep disappeared from view as it descended. When her SUV reached the top of the hill, she saw the Jeep, which was no longer moving. The driver's-side door had been flung open.

She didn't see the driver anywhere, and there was no indication of which direction he might have gone. Narrowing her eyes and leaning forward, she stared through the windshield. Her heart was still racing from the adrenaline rush of the pursuit.

"There," said Trevor.

Her gaze followed the direction Trevor pointed. A man in a khaki windbreaker and hat disappeared behind a rock formation.

There was no time to radio Chase and let him know what was going on.

She drove the patrol car to where the other car had been abandoned, due to the terrain being too rough to drive over. She and Trevor jumped out of the SUV, and Hannah deployed Captain. She headed toward the rocks with Trevor keeping pace with her. Hannah drew her gun as they ran. They entered a huge rocky field containing plenty of big boulders that someone could hide behind.

They slowed, taking time to look for movement and listen for any sound that might indicate which direction the driver had gone. Her heart-beat thrummed in her ears and sweat trickled past her temples as they advanced deeper into the rocky field. She could see where the field ended and opened up into a forest of scrubby trees— beyond that was the lake.

A flash of movement above a large rock, like a bird fluttering low to the ground, drew her atten-tion. She ran toward where she thought the man might be. When she saw him head toward the forest of short trees with tangled trunks, her sus-picion was confirmed. Beneath the hat he wore, she couldn't see his face clearly. From this dis-tance, he looked shorter than the RMK.

She ran ahead of Trevor while Captain kept pace with her. The man disappeared into the for-est.

The forest grew denser with the trees not al-lowing her to see much beyond the tangled branches, even though many of the leaves had fallen to the ground. It was like peering through lattice. She stopped and Trevor came up beside her. Captain remained still while she listened for any noise that might tell her which direction the man had gone.

Her breathing seemed to grow louder in the silence. Both of them were gasping for air from sprinting.

A sudden rush of noise, breaking branches and the pounding of footsteps indicated which direction they should go. Pushing branches aside, they darted through the forest and reached a place where the trees were farther apart, opening up to tall grass and brush, and beyond that the beach that led to the lake.

As she scanned the landscape, she saw no sign of the man in the khaki coat. The brush provided a few places to hide and his neutral-colored clothes would camouflage him. She was fully aware that he might have a gun.

She lifted her firearm and took several steps through the grass. Captain brushed against her thigh as he heeled beside her. Though the dog was not trained to track, he had some natural skills and would signal with a muted bark if he thought danger was close.

Trevor squeezed her arm and pointed at a bush. He must have noticed something. Treading lightly, they advanced through the grass.

As they drew near to the spot where Trevor had pointed, several birds flew up from the brush. The sudden movement and noise made her heart beat faster as she took a step back.

"Sorry," whispered Trevor. "I saw the branches moving and assumed it was a person."

"It's okay." She was already turning in a half circle, trying to figure out where the man had gone. He had to be hiding somewhere in the grass and brush. Once he headed toward the beach, he'd be easy enough to spot. So maybe he was choosing to stay in place.

A soft breeze rustled around the three of them as they stood still. The shrill cries of birds in the distance filled the air. Hannah scanned the area around her several times, looking for any sign of the man.

"I don't think we're going to find him today." Trevor kept his voice low. "Somehow, he got away."

Or he had found a good hiding spot.

She didn't want to give up, but Trevor was probably right. If he was still close, the man wasn't going to move as long as he thought he might get caught.

Maybe they could flush him out if he thought they were leaving. She turned to head back up the hill, glancing backward several times but still not seeing any signs of the man.

When they came to the Jeep, Hannah stopped to check the registration after noticing that the license plates were for Wyoming. Interesting. The paperwork in the glove box said the car belonged to Anise Withers. She wasn't sure what local resources Chase could tap into, but maybe the car could be brought in as evidence and checked for fingerprints. Certainly, Isla could trace the registration and Anise would be contacted to find out how she was related to the man they had just pursued.

They returned to her patrol vehicle and loaded

up Captain. She radioed Chase to let him know what had happened. "I doubt he'll return to the Jeep, but we can watch it for a bit, out of sight."

Chase responded, "Give it a few minutes. I'm looking at a map of the area you're in. We're on the road he might have run out to and there is no sight of a man on foot."

"He found somewhere to hide out," said Hannah.

"If you think you got this handled, Ian and I are close to the causeway. We're going to load up on some food for the team in Syracuse."

"Ten-four." Hannah lifted her finger off the talk button.

After they watched the Jeep for some time, seeing no sign of the man, she drove back toward the trailhead parking lot and then out to the main road. Though her food had gone cold, she munched on fries just to fill the hole in her stomach.

She was pretty sure the man who had evaded them was the same one who had come after her at the lake. He seemed to have some knowledge of the island. The only thing that didn't fit was the Wyoming license plates.

When they arrived at the ranch, they found Isla at her computers. She looked up from her screen. "Tough break. Chase told me what happened."

"We almost had him." Hannah slumped down on the couch and let out a heavy breath. Captain lay down at her feet. "I assume Chase and Ian are still out getting groceries?"

While staring at the screen in front of her, Isla ran her fingers through her dark hair. "Yes, I think he said something about meeting Meadow in Syracuse as well."

"Right, Chase said he was going to have her come over from Salt Lake now that it looks like the RMK is staying on the island."

Trevor sat down on the other end of the couch. He leaned his head back and closed his eyes, clearly exhausted. Maybe now he would see the wisdom of staying under guard at the ranch. She hoped Chase would let her go out with the rest of the team if she didn't have to take him along.

Hannah pulled out her scrunchie from where it had drifted down her head. She gathered the stray strands of her hair together to create a tidier bun. "Can you run a name for me? Anise Withers. That's who the green Jeep is registered to. The Jeep has Wyoming plates. I wonder if there is any connection to Elk Valley."

Isla pulled her chair closed to the table and tapped her keyboard. "That's easy enough." She looked at her screen. "Just give me a second. Here we go." She leaned closer to the screen. "The car is from Laramie and was reported stolen from Antelope Park about an hour ago."

"Where from?"

"The visitors' center," said Isla.

"So that means Anise was probably a tourist here on the island who had had her car stolen. No connection to the guy who came after us." The information seemed to confirm her theory that the driver in the green Jeep was the man who wanted her dead.

A shiver ran down her spine. Jodie's killer was still out there, and he had been clever enough to acquire a car that wouldn't be traced back to him.

Trevor felt the fatigue settle into his bones. It was a good kind of tired, though like a day spent baling hay or fencing. It was rewarding to be helping make progress on the RMK case. Hannah was probably disappointed they hadn't been able to bring in the man in the green Jeep. Catching him would mean her life would no longer be under threat and she could focus on her work. She would get her life back.

There was a part of him that felt like his own life had been taken from him ten years ago. Guilt over the death of his friends had suspended him in time. He hadn't moved on. He should be married and with kids by now and yet, his friends had never been given that chance.

Isla tapped away on her keyboard. "While you two were out and about, I was pulling up and compiling pictures of park employees."

Hannah rose to her feet. "Where did you find

those? Don't you have to have permission to get employee records?"

"Yes," said Isla. "But the website is free to access, and most list their employees along with a photograph."

Hannah peered over Isla's shoulder. Trevor stood up, as well, and walked toward the screen.

"Give me a second," said Isla. "I'll eliminate the obvious ones that don't fit." She kept typing. "We are looking for a male under forty, medium build, brown curly hair." She lifted her hands from the keyboard and pushed back her chair. "It's all yours. I'm going to grab a bite to eat. We brought a little food with us this morning."

She retreated to the kitchen.

Trevor offered the chair to Hannah while he stood behind her. He leaned close enough that he smelled her floral perfume. The first photo came on the screen. A man with straight, dark brown hair and intense brown eyes.

"You saw him up close and for longer than I did," said Trevor. "But I just don't think that is the guy."

She studied the photo. "He could have changed his hairstyle, but I think you're right. The face is too symmetrical. The guy I saw wasn't good-looking." An image flashed through her mind. "His chin was pointed, and his eyes were close together."

They clicked through several more photos, shaking their heads each time.

Isla returned holding a sandwich on a paper plate. "Anything?"

"Not so far," said Trevor.

"Bear in mind that some of those photos might be older. I'm not sure how often the park updates their website." She took a bite of her sandwich. "It could be that he's a new hire. He might have transferred from another area around the lake that utilizes park rangers. I can do a search on those, too." Isla took a seat on the couch.

They filed through the last few photos. Hannah slumped back in her chair. Trevor squeezed her shoulder. "We'll find him."

Her hand brushed over his where it rested on her shoulder, sending a surge of warmth through him.

"I hope so," she said. "Remember what that ranger at the visitors' center said. That he didn't think anyone was assigned to pick up trash in that area?"

"Yes," said Trevor.

"What if he went back there because it's where Jodie died? He just needed the excuse of picking up the trash to revisit the place. He might go there often."

Trevor shook his head. "I don't quite get what you're saying."

Isla rose to her feet and tossed her paper plate

in the trash. "I think I know what you're getting at, Hannah. Sometimes killers keep trophies or mementos of their crime and sometimes they go back to the place where it happened."

Hannah shuddered. "Kind of creepy."

"But he won't be going back there now that he knows he'll be recognized," said Trevor.

"You're probably right about that," said Isla.

Hannah's words came out haltingly. "But he'll stay around here until he can get to me."

Isla patted her friend's shoulder. "Why don't you give me that chair, and I'll see what other places around the lake have websites with employee pictures."

"I need to take Captain out for his walk, anyway." Hannah rose to her feet. Captain stood up from where he'd been lying on a rug, then wagged his tail and looked at her expectantly. The dog understood what she'd said.

"I'll go with you," said Trevor.

"I almost forgot." Hannah walked toward Isla and pulled a piece of paper out of her pocket. "That's the license plate of a white compact car that we noticed a couple of times. It might be nothing, but you got to follow every lead, right?"

"I can run it for you. No problem."

Trevor waited for Hannah after pushing the door open.

As they stepped out the door, Hannah commented, "Let's stay to the areas where there aren't very many tourists."

"Sounds like a plan," he said.

The ranch had plenty of open area with grass and trees, in addition to the numerous buildings and barns. They walked past a narrow three-sided barn that contained old trucks and tractors, and out toward a field surrounded by trees. He could just make out a barbed-wire fence in the distance. Some of the trees still had gold, red and yellow leaves on them.

"Isla seems nice," he said. "She certainly knows her stuff."

"I've enjoyed working with her. She's from Elk Valley. You never met her?"

He shook his head. "She may have moved there after I left. I know Elk Valley is only six thousand people, but I still didn't know everyone."

"She's been through a lot in the last few months," said Hannah.

"Really?"

"She's been trying to foster a child so she can adopt. An anonymous person called the agency and told lies about her being unfit to be a foster mom. Last month, someone set her house on fire. They never caught who did it, though we're pretty sure it's the same person who tried to discredit her with the foster agency."

"That is so unfair. Any inkling of who might be behind all that?"

Hannah shook her head. "I know she looked into ex-boyfriends and a cousin who was mad at her. But so far, she hasn't found anything solid. The team is doing as much as they can to help her. I hope things get resolved. She would be a great foster mom."

They came to a freshwater creek. The trickling of the water over rocks was soothing to Trevor. Captain stood on the bank his focus on Hannah.

Hannah waved her arm in a half circle. "Dive in."

Captain lumbered into the creek and splashed around. He put his head down to get a drink and then splashed some more.

"Man, he loves the water." Trevor laughed.

"Newfoundlands are natural swimmers. They even have webbed feet," she said.

The giant fur ball of a dog romped through the water. Hannah tossed a stick into the river and Captain dove for it.

Watching the dog play lifted a weight off his own shoulders. Judging from the smile on her face, the moment was doing the same for Hannah.

Hannah commanded Captain to get out of the water. Once on the bank, he shook his big wooly body, spraying droplets of water everywhere. They both stepped back to avoid getting wet.

In her haste, Hannah crashed into Trevor and stepped on his boot. The back of her head collided with his face.

She whirled around and gazed up at him. "I'm sorry."

He bent toward her and touched her arm. "No problem." She was near enough for him to feel her body heat as he looked into her green eyes. He found himself bending closer.

Both of them took a step back at the same time. As heat rose up his neck, he turned sideways and studied the rippling creek. What had that been about? He'd almost kissed her.

Hannah patted her bun and the back of her head with a nervous energy. She shot a sideways glance at him.

Captain let out a woof—maybe he'd picked up on the electric charge that had just passed between him and Hannah.

Hannah kneeled down and rubbed his head. "You big old teddy bear."

Captain returned the affection with some kisses on Hannah's cheeks.

Grateful that Captain had broken the intensity of the moment, Trevor stepped closer to rub Captain's ear. "What a good boy." As he leaned down, his shoulder brushed against hers. Even a brief touch reignited the warmth he'd experienced a moment before.

Several people had come out into the field where they were.

Hannah watched the group of five people for a moment. "We should probably go back inside."

He glanced over his shoulder as they headed back toward the three-sided barn. There were two men in the group, one of whom was wearing a hat that concealed his face. The other man was the right build to be Hannah's assailant, but his hair was black. He doubted the guy would show himself in such an obvious way. The arrival of the people milling around was a reminder that they could not take any chances. It would be easy enough for the RMK or the other man to hide in a crowd of tourists.

SEVEN

When they returned to the community room, both Chase and Ian were unloading groceries from the backs of their vehicles. Dash and Lola sat dutifully by the front door. Both dogs, the golden retriever and the German shepherd, held their heads high and sniffed the air, tuning into their surroundings.

Officer Meadow Ames pulled up in her vehicle, as well. Meadow got out and released Grace, a vizsla, from her kennel. She followed the dog while it wandered, sniffed and did her business. Because of her tracking skills, the dog should be useful to the investigation.

With a bright smile on her face, Meadow waved at Ian as he went inside with the load of groceries. The two of them had fallen in love and gotten engaged a few months ago.

Trevor and Hannah helped bring in the groceries. As the four of them carried the bags into the kitchen, she was grateful to have other people around. The tender moment between her and

Trevor by the creek still had her rattled. Was it possible to be attracted to someone who you weren't sure you even liked.? And Trevor certainly was that. It wasn't just his obstinance about being protected, but the story of what he had done to Naomi ten years ago that still echoed through her brain. Perhaps her own mistreatment from men, cheating and being stood up, colored her judgement. All the same, if there was even a small chance Trevor was that kind of guy, it wasn't worth getting hurt again.

Chase placed a can of tomatoes, and some packages of hamburger and sausage on the counter. "I got all the stuff for spaghetti. Any volunteers to help out?"

"Rocco is a really good cook. Especially Italian," said Hannah.

"He and Selena should be back anytime now, but I need to get this sauce started," said Chase. "Maybe he can add his special touch and secret ingredients once I get it simmering."

Hannah put her grocery bag on the counter and peered inside. "Looks like you got ingredients for salad and garlic toast. I can help make those."

Trevor moved closer to Hannah. "I'll give you a hand with that."

Chase nodded. "You can prep that stuff if you want to, but the sauce will need to simmer through the afternoon."

Feeling a tightening in her chest, she pressed

her lips together. She'd hoped that Trevor would go back into the living room, where Ian, Meadow and Isla were, so she didn't have to contend with the feelings of attraction every time he was close.

"Tomatoes and lettuce are in the bag at the end of the counter," said Chase.

She looked at Trevor momentarily. The eye contact made her heart flutter. She turned toward the cupboards. "I'll see if I can find you a knife and cutting board."

Chase opened a drawer by the stove and handed her a knife. It took her only a moment to retrieve a cutting board and a large bowl, which she sat by Trevor.

"I'll get the bread ready to broil," she said.

"I'm just glad this kitchen was stocked with some basics," said Chase. "There should be some vinegar and oil to make a dressing."

The kitchen filled with the smell of browning meat.

As she buttered the bread and put garlic and Parmesan cheese on it, she was keenly aware of Trevor's proximity. He sliced through the tomatoes with expertise. They finished the rest of the meal prep.

Hannah avoided Trevor for the rest of the afternoon.

By the time dinner was ready, Rocco and Selena had returned from their search for the RMK.

Chase greeted them as he carried a steaming

pot of spaghetti sauce toward the table. "Dinner will give us a chance to debrief as a team."

Hannah set the bread on the table.

"Smells wonderful," said Meadow.

The rest of the food was placed on the table, then everyone took a seat and Chase said grace. Trevor sat across from her, next to Rocco.

After all the food had been passed around the table and everyone's plates were full, Chase addressed his comments to Selena and Rocco. Both of them were slumped over, as though that day had been a long one.

"Did you find out anything more about the RMK?"

They shook their heads in unison.

"Nothing solid," said Selena. "It sounds like Hannah got the strongest lead."

Rocco tore a piece of garlic toast in half. "So, are we going to stake out that campground tonight?"

"Yes," said Chase, "but we can't show up in our patrol cars. I asked around. The ranch has a van they use for tours that they can loan us. Ian, Meadow and Selena will be going with me. Two people will remain in the vehicle and two will be on foot."

"Hannah's not going? It's her lead," said Rocco.

"I think it would be better if she stayed behind with Trevor," said Chase.

Her stomach clenched. She didn't like being kept from the action of the investigation.

"Rocco, you'll stay here as well to stand guard through the night, so get a few hours sleep after dinner." Chase glanced over at Hannah. "Hannah will brief you on what happened with her and Trevor today."

Rocco nodded. "I heard a little bit from Isla. That same guy came after you in a car. Sounds like a cold case that just heated up." His voice was filled with compassion. "I'm sorry they never caught the guy who killed your friend."

Hannah shook her head as she set down her fork. "I didn't remember his face until I saw him again."

Trevor added, "He works for the park service."

After dinner and cleanup, Chase and the other three left to set up the stakeout. The sky had already turned gray. This late in the fall, it got dark shortly after dinner.

"I'm going to get that rest Chase suggested." Rocco squeezed Hannah's shoulder as he walked past her. "Wake me in a couple hours so I can take over guard duty."

Hannah listened to Rocco's retreating footsteps as he moved toward the outside door in the kitchen, the fastest way to get to the bunkhouse. Cocoa followed beside him. Isla had already excused herself and gone to the bunkhouse.

Trevor sat opposite her on one of the couches.

He glanced around. "Now what?" His voice was filled with expectation.

The way he gazed at her caused her breath to catch. At the same time, she wanted to run very far away. Somehow, they had ended up alone together. "I need to take Captain for a walk."

He lifted himself from the sofa. "I'll go with you."

"I think it would be safer if you stayed here inside."

"You shouldn't go out by yourself, either," he said. "Maybe you should wait until Rocco wakes up."

"I'm a trained officer." She didn't want to be alone with Trevor and these blossoming feelings. "I can't *not* take him out. Stay inside. I won't be long." Her words held a force to them.

With Captain heeling beside her, she stepped outside, switched on her flashlight and broke into a run. The exercise was more for her to get rid of some of her twisted-up emotions than for Captain. As her feet pounded the dirt road, the dog kept pace with her, not questioning what she was doing.

The sprint left her breathless, but the burst of activity made her feel less tied up in knots. She bent over, resting her hands on her knees. Captain wandered into the tall grass to do his business.

Once he was done, she walked back toward the community room and bunkhouse. No exterior lights illuminated the outside of the community room. A warm glow emanated from the two visible windows. An undulating shadow caught her attention as it disappeared around the side of the building.

Was someone skulking around the building? She ran back to the community room and opened the door. Trevor's laptop was open on the couch, but there was no sign of him.

She drew her gun and hurried outside praying that nothing had happened to Trevor.

Trevor retreated toward the bunkhouse, where he'd left his gun. He'd seen shadows at one of the windows. When he'd run to the door, he thought he heard footsteps. Someone was out there.

As he'd stood on the threshold, he couldn't see Hannah's flashlight in the distance. Had something happened to her?

He entered the bunkhouse, where Rocco was snoring, grabbed his gun from the drawer where he'd put it and stepped outside.

A voice shouted at him from the darkness. "Police. Stop right there."

"Hannah?"

She stepped out of the shadows. "What are you doing out here?" She holstered her weapon.

"I heard a noise and thought I saw someone."

"I told you to stay inside." Her voice was filled with irritation.

"I was worried about you." Why was she so defensive? Couldn't she see he was trying to protect her?

Her voice softened slightly. "I appreciate the gesture, but I can take care of myself."

She stared down at the gun in his hand. "What are you doing with that? Chase told you not to use it. It's bad enough you won't just go to a safe house. You don't need to get into a gun battle and end up dead."

He let out a heavy sigh. "I have a right to protect myself. I thought I could help you."

"Go back to your room and stay there with the door locked. You'll be safe in there with Rocco. I'm going to check the perimeter of the building." Each word was enunciated and delivered with intensity.

"I'm sorry." His words had some punch to them. The way she spoke made it sound like she was ordering him around.

"Why can't you just do what Chase says and what I say? Can't you see we're trying to keep you alive?"

"Yes, I know that." A note of irritation entered his voice.

"Captain and I will be back in a few minutes. I'll knock on the door and say your name."

Feeling like an errant schoolboy, he retreated to the bunkhouse. After placing the gun on the table by the twin bed, he locked the door and sat down on the bed. It didn't seem to matter to her that his motive was to make sure she was okay.

She probably hadn't even felt the magnetic connection that had passed between them at the creek. He stared at the ceiling. The intense emotion had probably been driven by all the time they were spending together and the lightness of the moment. Resting his elbows on his knees, he placed his head in his hands. Had it all been in his imagination?

At least five minutes passed, and she didn't return. The room had only one window that looked out on the open field, and the trees and fence beyond.

Both of them thought they had seen someone outside the community room. Maybe that someone had been scared off, or maybe he was still lurking around, waiting for an opportunity.

He walked to the door and twisted the dead bolt so he could peer out. He wondered if he should wake Rocco but thought better of it. If he was going to be on guard duty all night, he needed his rest. This could be a false alarm. He hadn't heard the sound of a struggle or gunshots. It just seemed like she should be back by now.

He was torn between doing what she said and making sure she was safe. He wasn't sure why she was so resistant to his offer of help. Staring into the darkness, he took several steps away from the door.

He heard Captain barking in the distance and then saw a flashlight bobbing up and down, coming back toward the bunkhouse.

Trevor hurried back inside, locked the door and sat down on the bed.

A moment later, he heard a knock on the door. "Trevor, it's me."

He rose and opened the door. The noise had not awakened Rocco.

"Thank you for staying inside."

Not wanting to lie, he didn't say anything or even nod.

"Let's go back to the community room," she whispered.

He trailed behind her. They entered the quiet space. He sat down where he'd left his laptop. "Did you see anything?"

"I thought I saw movement by one of the barns. All the tourists should be gone by now. This place closes down a little after the dinner hour." Hannah paced the room, peering out each window.

"We both thought we saw a person moving around the outside of the building. I think someone was here."

"I agree," she said. "What we don't know is if he is still around or if it someone dangerous or just a tourist trying to have an after-hours look at the place." Hannah still hadn't sat down. Captain followed her with his eyes. With her hands on her hips, she stopped at one of the windows and peered out.

Guilt got the better of him. "Hannah, I have something to confess."

She turned to look at him. "Yes?"

"I left the bunkhouse for a moment. I only took a few steps outside. I was worried about you when you didn't come back."

"You shouldn't have done that." She sat down on the sofa opposite him. "I appreciate your honesty."

"Why does it bother you so much that I want to help keep *you* safe?"

She stared at the floor for a moment before looking at him. "Because it makes me feel like you think I can't do my job."

Her answer shocked him. "I never said that."

"You didn't have to." She sounded defensive.

"I don't like you assuming things about me. You don't know what's going on in my head." With each exchange, both their voices got louder.

With that stern look on her face, she opened her mouth as if to say something, then shook her head, stood up and walked away.

Captain made a groaning noise and lay down on the floor.

The moment of silence seemed to have calmed them both. "I don't want to get in an argument with you, Hannah."

She turned back around to face him. "It's just

that I thought this assignment would go very differently. I pictured myself coming out here and convincing you to do in person what Chase couldn't get you to do over the phone, go to a safe house. I had no way of knowing that the first time we met I would be so...compromised because of what happened to me."

"Hannah, you have to let yourself be human. Anyone who had almost been drowned would have been...upset."

The tightness in her jaw and the hard angles of her features seemed to soften. "Thank you for saying that."

"I imagine your job is not an easy one. You have to deal with all kinds of difficult people and maintain control."

"Yes, that's true, and sometimes those people have had too much to drink or are bigger and stronger than me."

"I'm not trying to be one of those people. I just want to help catch the RMK. I feel an obligation," he said.

"I get that, but I don't want you to end up hurt or worse on my watch."

"I'm glad we had this conversation." He felt like he was seeing Hannah more clearly. She was a woman with a strong sense of responsibility and a desire to do her job well. The attacks on her had made her feel insecure about her abilities.

"Me, too." She headed toward the kitchen. "I

think I saw some root beer in the fridge. You want one?"

"Sure," he said. They seemed to have at least called a truce.

Hannah returned and handed him a can. She sat down and took a few sips of her drink. He opened his laptop. He hadn't gotten much work done today. He read through a report he'd written about how a ranch he was a consultant on could expand their operation without adding much debt one more time before sending it. When he looked up, Hannah had closed her eyes and was resting her head against the back of the couch with her arms crossed over her chest.

"I'm not asleep," she said. "I'm just resting."

She must be tired. She couldn't have gotten much sleep while guarding him last night.

"You could tell I was staring at you without opening your eyes?"

She opened one eye. "Of course. I'm not going to fall asleep while I'm on guard duty." Her voice held a lighter tone that he had not heard before.

"I could use some sleep myself," he said. "It's been a long day."

She checked her watch. "Let's give Rocco a little more time. I'll wake him up, so I can get some rest. He'll be stationed outside your door and I'll just be next door."

They waited another hour in the community

room. Trevor gave up trying to work and closed his laptop.

Hannah rose to her feet. "Let's go. It's been a long day."

She and Captain escorted Trevor outside and walked to the bunkhouse. After waking Rocco, Trevor collapsed on the bed without changing out of his clothes. Sleep came quickly until he was jolted awake by the cacophony of frantically barking dogs. They had an intruder.

EIGHT

At the sound of Captain's barking, Hannah awoke with a start. The Newfoundland stood by the door. Outside, she could hear Cocoa barking, as well. After peeling back her covers, she jumped up and grabbed her gun belt. She'd slept in her clothes for this very reason—if an intruder tried to breach the security of the bunkhouse.

The other twin bed was still empty. The rest of the team must still be out on surveillance. Isla hadn't come to bed either though there were no lights on in the community room.

Captain continued to bark as she slipped on her shoes.

Two intense knocks on her door reverberated through the tiny room.

Rocco spoke with a staccato rhythm. "Intruder. I think he went toward the field where those trees are. I'm headed to check it out."

Hannah tied her shoelaces and bolted across the floor to click Captain into his leash. "Got it. I'll stay close to Trevor."

She swung open the door and stepped outside in time to see Rocco disappearing into the darkness. Trevor stood outside his room. His hair was disheveled, and he was bleary-eyed. "Trouble?"

"Yes, get back inside." She stepped toward his room.

A gunshot resounded through the air. Hannah leaped toward Trevor, taking him to the ground. The bullet had shattered the light above the bunkhouse. They were in darkness.

Hannah had taken off her shoulder radio to sleep and hadn't had time to reattach it. She had no way to let Rocco know the assailant was still close to the bunkhouse. Maybe he had been close enough to hear the shot.

She rolled off Trevor, who crawled toward the open door of his room. Another shot whizzed by him.

She could just make out Trevor putting a protective hand toward his head. "That was close," he shout-whispered.

"He's got a line on you. You won't make it to the room before being shot. This way." She crawled toward the side of the community room, which would provide cover. The shooter would have to reposition to get a shot at them from this side of the building. Trevor came up beside her, and both of them pressed their backs against the wall. Captain panted and leaned close to her.

Isla was suddenly beside Trevor. "I have the key to the community room. I locked it up when I went for a walk."

"Good idea. Let's get inside. I can radio Rocco from there." The community room, which had two exits, would be safer than the bunkhouse room, which had only the one door for escape if the shooter chose to close in.

They moved along the outside wall and turned the corner where the door was. Isla edged in front of Hannah and pulled a key out of her pocket. In the dim light, she had to bend close to the knob to see.

Hannah pulled her gun and peered out into the inky night.

Isla and Trevor slipped in through the back door, entering the dark kitchen.

"Stay low, so we're not seen through the window." Hannah studied the area outside one final time. Not seeing or hearing anything, she followed the other two inside, locking the door behind her. Captain remained at her heels.

Crouching, they rushed past the counter into the living room. Isla turned on a single light. Hannah grabbed the radio and pressed the talk button. "Intruder is believed to be close to the premises. We're in the community room."

"Thought I heard shots. On my way back," Rocco responded.

"Exercise caution. Two shots fired from the

north side of the building. That doesn't mean our perp is staying in one place."

"Got it. I'm going to see if Cocoa can track him." Hannah wasn't sure if that would work. Cocoa's training was for arson.

"We'll stay put," said Hannah.

Isla and Trevor had already taken up a position on the floor, their backs resting against the sofa. She kept the gun in her hand as she peered over the back of the couch out the window. She could barely discern the trees from the dark sky.

Still crouching, she proceeded to get closer to the window, lifting her head just a little above the sill and watching. She peered out several other windows, not seeing any sign of the person who had taken shots at them. He must be using a night scope to have gotten so close to hitting his target after the bunkhouse light was shattered.

Captain sat several feet from her, his head held high as if waiting for a command. She checked the other windows again. She should have seen Rocco and Cocoa by now or at least a bobbing flashlight. They couldn't have gotten far in such a short amount of time.

"Anything?" Trevor asked. He'd lifted his head just above the sofa.

Something must have happened to Rocco. "I'm going out there. Lock the door behind me."

Before Trevor could object, she and Captain hurried to the front door. She stepped outside.

She pressed against the building and peered out toward the barns and outbuildings. On the other side of the door, the bolt slid into place.

The sound of a dog's intense barking reached her ears. She and Captain sprinted in the direction of the noise through the darkness.

As her feet pounded through the grass and over the hard ground, she was aware that she could be running into an ambush. Slowing, she looked side to side.

The glow of a flashlight in the grass caught her eye. She sprinted toward it. The sound of the water rippling over rocks reached her ears. She was by the creek she and Trevor had been at earlier. The barking grew more intense, and she could see Cocoa pacing. The chocolate Lab was barely visible but for her K-9 vest.

When her eyes adjusted to the darkness, she saw that Rocco was lying on the ground by the dropped flashlight. She rushed toward him.

Before she could reach him, a force grabbed her from behind and dragged her toward the creek. Weight pulled her down and her feet grew wet. She saw flashes of a face, and brown curly hair, then he pushed her under and held her there with one hand on her neck and the other on her torso. The weight of the utility belt dragged her under.

She whipped her head back and forth while trying to pry his hand off her neck. With her other hand, she managed to pull her baton and hit his arm with it repeatedly. The pressure on her body let up enough that she was able to lift her head. She gasped for air before being pushed under again. This time, his hand was on her shoulder. His other hand braced the arm that held the baton so she could not get enough arc to hit him again.

She wasn't going to die tonight at this man's hands, not when he should be in jail. Unable to see clearly, she grasped at the first thing she could get hold of, his shirt. She pulled him closer and then reached up, this time scratching his face. The man pulled back. She was able to get into a sitting position and hit him hard across the stomach.

He fell backward into the water. With the water rippling around her, she rose to her feet and raised the baton as he crawled toward the bank.

Captain had jumped in, blocking the man's easy escape route.

Wading through the calf-deep rushing water, Hannah prepared to land a blow.

The man turned on her suddenly, pulling a gun from a holster. "Back off or I'll shoot the dog."

Hannah put both hands in the air. She wasn't about to lose her partner. She called Captain toward her.

Still pointing the gun at her, the man glanced toward the buildings before crawling up the bank. He rose to his feet. Her breath caught. Was he going to shoot her? Once he was standing, he turned and took off running toward the trees.

Weighed down by wet clothes, Hannah dragged herself through the water and up the bank where the man had gone. She glanced over her shoulder, where she saw a bobbing light moving toward her. Trevor, maybe, or Isla. That must be why the man ran. He didn't want witnesses or to contend with more people. Yet, he had the gun all along. Why go to the trouble of trying to drown her?

An agitated Cocoa paced and whined beside his partner who lay motionless on the ground.

Please, God, don't let Rocco be shot.

She couldn't see much in the darkness. She shook Rocco's shoulder and said his name but got no response. She touched his neck.

Cocoa moved in closer and licked Hannah's cheek, as if to show support.

She let out a breath when she felt a pulse.

"Is he all right?" Isla asked as she came up behind her. Her flashlight didn't reveal any blood around Rocco.

"I don't think he's shot, just unconscious." Had he been used as bait to get Hannah close to the creek?

"You stay here with Rocco." She patted Isla's forearm. She had a suspect to catch. She took off running with Captain by her side.

Exhausted from her fight and weighed down by wet clothes, she willed herself to run in the direction the man had gone but did not get far before she slowed to catch her breath.

Trevor caught up with her. His hand rested on her soaking shirt. "I saw you running and came to help."

No matter what she said, it was clear that Trevor was going to be an active part of this investigation and right now she needed him to be.

"Your timing is perfect." She pointed in the direction the man had run. "He went that way."

"Got it." Trevor bolted ahead of her.

"Trevor!" she called after him. Despite that it was against protocol, she was grateful that he had come to assist her but was afraid for his safety.

She struggled to keep up as he disappeared into the darkness. She ran in the direction he'd gone.

A single gunshot filled the air. But it had not come from the trees where the man had gone. Instead, it seemed to have been fired toward where the barns and other buildings were.

She turned abruptly and sprinted toward where the shot had been fired, praying that she wasn't too late.

Upon hearing a gunshot, Trevor had sought cover behind one of the old trucks in the three-sided barn. The man who had assaulted Hannah had doubled back and run into the heart of the ranch, slipping between the buildings. Leaving his flashlight turned off and moving with a light step, Trevor had been stealthy enough to not be detected until they were close to the buildings. When the assailant had noticed him, he immediately took a shot, which went wild in the darkness. The next bullet might find its mark, though, if the guy got close enough.

Trevor crouched down behind the truck bed.

He could hear slow-moving footsteps. The man was searching for him and getting closer. Without a gun, Trevor had only the element of surprise on his side. If the guy got close enough, he might be able to jump him.

A threatening voice cut through the darkness. "You're in the way."

The words chilled Trevor to the bone. Judging from how loud the voice was, the man was very close. Trevor had gone after him thinking he only wanted to kill Hannah. His words indicated that he saw Trevor as an expendable obstacle.

Trevor's heartbeat thrummed in his ears. Staying in a crouched position strained his leg muscles. The seconds between footsteps seemed to drag on. Then the padding of footfalls on packed dirt grew fainter.

He took in a breath. The assailant had moved past him without noticing his hiding place.

"Stop—police."

A shot reverberated through the air. Trevor lifted his head above the truck bed in time to see

Hannah race by with Captain at her side headed in the same direction the culprit had gone.

He fell in behind her. Hannah looked over her shoulder at him just as he caught up. He scanned the darkness up ahead but didn't see anything. Hannah slowed, then stopped to look around.

She patted his arm. "Glad you're okay," she whispered.

They were nearly to the orientation building, which was locked up and dark.

He glanced around before edging closer to Hannah and Captain.

"Careful." His muscles tensed as he searched the darkness.

There were plenty of possible hiding places where the guy could take a shot at them. Still, Captain would bark if the man was close.

Though he could no longer see the fleeing man, Trevor headed in the most likely direction he would have gone, toward the entrance to the ranch.

When they got to the parking lot, it was empty.

He couldn't hear anything, no car starting up or speeding away. "He must have parked his car somewhere around here, and that's why he had to come back through the farm."

Hannah still held her gun, though she dropped her hand to her side. She glanced down at Captain, who remained still. "If Captain doesn't sense that he's close, it means we lost him." She put her gun in the holster.

They trudged back through the farm.

"It's good you came when you did to help me chase the suspect, but you put yourself in danger," she said.

He was glad that she was accepting his help. "I don't mind. I'm in danger no matter what. We can work together on this. I want to catch that guy as much as you do. I want this to be over for you Hannah."

"You know how I feel about the RMK," she said. "I want it to be over for you too."

"Maybe we can help each other end both our nightmares."

"We're sort of up against the same thing."

Though the suggestion had been made before, it was the first time since their meeting that he sensed she had softened toward the idea of him aiding in the investigation.

"It's strange. He had a gun. Once I was out in the open searching for Rocco, he could have just shot me. Instead, he drags me to the creek."

"Something about this guy and water, huh?"

Hannah's shoes made soft squishing noises as they walked on the trail around the multiple buildings. The sliding door on one of the barns had been left open, revealing the darkness from within and reminding him of how and where so many of his friends had died. So far, the RMK had not made a move on him.

"Most murderers tend to use the same MO over and over," she said.

As they approached, light glowed from within the community room while the part of the bunk-house he could see was still dark. "So the guy is fixated on drowning people?"

"It could indicate some deeper psychological stuff that might be important. I've only had a little training in behavioral profiling, so I am not sure what is going on here," she said.

He reached for the door of the community room. When he jiggled the handle, it was locked.

Hannah knocked. "Isla, it's Hannah and Trevor."

Isla came to the door and opened it. Her expression, the raised eyebrows and bent neck, held a question.

Hannah shook her head as disappointment colored her words. "He got away."

Trevor let Hannah and Captain step across the threshold while he entered after they did.

In the community room, Rocco was sitting on one of the sofas with an ice pack pressed against the back of his head. Cocoa was lying at his feet.

Isla sat down in front of her monitors. "Just heard from Chase. They are calling off the stake-out. No sign of the RMK."

Hannah plunked down on the opposite end of

the couch from Rocco. "I take it you got knocked out."

Rocco nodded. "The guy came out of nowhere. I suspect I'm gonna have a bad headache in the morning. I'll go to Syracuse to be checked out soon as the sun comes up."

"I think he wanted to use you as bait to get me out there by the creek," said Hannah.

"Lot of premeditation in that," said Rocco.

Trevor peered out the window that offered a view of some of the farm buildings. The killers had something in common in that they both planned the murders to happen in a certain place, water and a barn. For the RMK, the barn must be symbolic. He wondered if that was true for the man who was after Hannah. He turned toward Isla. "Is there a reason why the guy would try to drown Hannah when shooting her would have been easier?"

Isla swung around in her office chair. "Sometimes killers want to recreate some trauma they themselves suffered."

Hannah leaned forward to stroke Captain's ear. "Like maybe he almost drowned once?"

"Or someone tried to drown him," said Isla.

Trevor settled on the couch opposite of where Hannah and Rocco were. It wasn't until he sat down that he realized how tired he was. His sleep had been interrupted. "You know, I think I want to go to bed."

Hannah turned toward Rocco. "You're probably not up for guard duty. I can take a post until the others get back from the stakeout. I have to change out of these wet clothes first."

Trevor shifted in his seat and ran his hands through his hair. "Do you think you should be out in the open like that, given what just happened?"

Hannah glanced in his direction but not with the usual look of challenge and defiance in her eyes. Instead he thought he read appreciation in her expression. "I suppose you're right. Maybe we should all just wait here and stay together until the rest of the team gets back."

With an injured officer and Hannah under threat herself, they were vulnerable.

Rocco rose to his feet. "I, for one, could eat some leftover spaghetti. Anyone else?"

"I'm good," said Isla. "Unless there is something a little lighter, like crackers or chips."

"I'll look," said Rocco.

As the room filled with the aroma of Italian spices, Trevor could feel his eyelids getting heavy. By the time the microwave dinged, he knew he wasn't going to last much longer.

The last thing he heard before he drifted off was the rustling of a potato-chip bag and Isla talking. "Hannah, if you want to come over, I have some more photos for you to look at."

He drifted off wondering if Isla had identified the man determined to kill Hannah.

NINE

After changing into dry clothes, Hannah grabbed a chair from the kitchen table and headed toward Isla's makeshift workstation. Trevor had fallen asleep with his head pressed on the armrest of the sofa. He looked serene and kind of cute when he slept.

She sat down by Isla. "I've pulled up more photos of park employees. I'll click through them—stop me if one catches your eye."

They filed through the photos. Each time Hannah shook her head. Only one even slightly looked like a possibility—a man with short buzz-cut hair. She leaned closer to the screen. "Do you suppose he's grown his hair out since this photo was taken and it gets curly when it's longer?"

"Could be," Isla said.

The face wasn't quite right. "I don't know." Then again, she'd only seen her attacker when he was enraged.

"We'll put him in the maybe file." Isla clicked through the remaining photos.

Hannah studied each picture carefully before shaking her head. When she glanced over at the sofa, Rocco had fallen asleep, as well. The soft hum of light snoring filled the room.

"If he works for the park service," said Isla. "He's got to be in the system somewhere. The next step is to have Chase put in the paperwork for me to have access to employee records."

"You think the guy might be a recent transfer? Jodie was killed eighteen years ago. He must be from around here even if he hasn't always worked on Antelope Island."

Isla shrugged. "Or his picture didn't make it onto the website for some other reason."

"Maybe he stole the uniform, and he wears it so no one questions why he's always down where Jodie died," said Hannah.

"It's a theory." Isla pushed a piece of paper toward her. "I almost forgot."

Hannah took the paper and saw that the name Florence Black was written on it. "The owner of the white compact car?"

"Does it ring any bells?"

Hannah put the paper in her pocket. "No, Florence sounds like an older woman's name."

"She's seventy, according to DMV records," said Isla.

She pointed at one of Isla's screens, unable to hide the disappointment in her voice. "Two dead ends. No photo and no clear connection to the car."

"Don't give up. We'll keep digging." Isla offered her a supportive smile as she pressed her shoulder against Hannah. Her attention was drawn to the two sleeping people. "Everyone looks like a younger version of themselves when they're sleeping." Her voice was wistful. "Like a child."

Isla had had a great deal of personal heartache from the time the task force had first congregated in Elk Valley in March. Other team members, and Isla herself, had filled in Hannah on her ongoing battle to foster a child and the damage that had been done to her reputation. "How are you doing with everything that has happened? I'm sure the house fire was unsettling after you had already been through so much."

Isla's fingers hovered over the keyboard as she let out a sigh. "Someone sure wants to ruin my life and steal my dreams of adopting a child. That much is clear. I just can't imagine who would do such a thing."

"Any word on the status of the little boy you put an application in to foster? What was his name?" From the other members of the team, Hannah had heard that Isla had previously been ready to foster a little girl when an anonymous caller told the agency that Isla would not be a fit mother because she drank and had a drug habit, a total lie. No doubt, this was the same person who had set fire to Isla's house in Elk Valley.

Isla pulled her purse toward her and took out her wallet. "His name is Enzo and I am hopeful that I will be chosen to foster him." She flipped open the wallet to a picture of a dark-haired little boy with an infectious smile.

"So sweet," said Hannah.

Isla closed the wallet. "Even though I've given up on meeting Mr. Right, I didn't think the dream of adopting would be so difficult." She yawned and pushed her chair back a few inches. "How about you? I don't remember you ever talking about a boyfriend."

"My life is pretty much work and being a good aunt to my nephew and niece. I don't have very good radar for picking decent men. They present themselves as good guys and turn out to be the exact opposite."

"I hear you," said Isla. Her gaze fell on the sleeping Trevor.

Isla was as familiar with the specifics of this investigation as she was. "Do you think he was telling the truth when he said he really liked Naomi?"

Before Isla could answer, there was knock on the front door. "That must be the rest of the team." Isla rose to her feet to unlock the door.

Chase, Ian, Selena and Meadow shuffled in. Their slumped shoulders and weighted features communicated extreme exhaustion.

Trevor and Rocco stirred awake.

While everyone else sat down, Chase remained standing. "I'll keep this brief since we're all tired. We know the RMK is here on the island. We don't know why he hasn't come after Trevor yet. We'll continue our search tomorrow. Get some sleep, everyone. Ian and Rocco, you're bunking with Trevor. We'll need to post a guard outside, as well."

Ian offered him a weary salute. "We'll figure it out."

Chase's attention was drawn to Rocco, who held the ice pack to his head.

"Did something happen here tonight?"

Hannah stepped forward. "We didn't have time to radio you, but the attacker came after me again tonight."

Shock spread across Chase's face. "That means he knows we have set up headquarters here."

Hannah nodded.

Chase rubbed his chin. "If we're to stay on the island, there are no other options for a place to stay overnight other than in RVs, an expense we can't afford."

"We'll just have to double down on security," said Rocco.

Chase nodded. "That's the best option. Can I get a volunteer to stand guard outside the bunkhouse to watch both Hannah's and Trevor's doors?"

Ian raised his hand. "I can do it, but I'm only going to last a couple of hours."

"I can take over after I've had a couple hours shut-eye," said Meadow.

Chase glanced at the clock on the wall. "We'll convene for breakfast and assignments at eight a.m."

That gave them only four hours to rest. They walked out in silence to their respective rooms. Isla and Meadow plopped down on the beds opposite Hannah. After removing her gun belt, she lay down fully clothed. In case there was another interruption in the night, she would be ready. Selena came a few minutes later, after she'd walked Scout. The dogs settled down by their owners' beds.

Sleep came quickly to Hannah, but her dreams were of being pulled under water and drifting down deeper and deeper.

She was awakened when Isla made a rustling around.

She lifted her head off the pillow. "What's going on?"

"Someone phoned into Chase. Another RMK sighting over at Ladyfinger campground."

Would Chase let her be part of the search? Still groggy, Hannah jumped to her feet and grabbed her gun belt. There was a better chance of him saying yes if she looked ready. "When did the call come in?"

"Two minutes ago," said Isla.

Hannah ran outside, where Meadow was sitting in a chair. Grace rested at her feet. She was still fastening her belt when Trevor stepped out of the other room. Ian came out a few seconds later.

Chase, who looked fully awake and was holding what must be coffee in a tumbler, stepped out of the back door of the community room. "We're down to four officers. I sent Rocco into town to get his injury checked out."

"You're down to five." Trevor stepped forward. "You have me. I want to help."

Hannah's stomach twisted tight. Taking him along could be a liability. Then again, she didn't want to be left behind to guard Trevor and be cut out of the action.

"He did help me chase the guy after me last night," she said. "I was glad to have the back-up."

Her breath caught in her throat as her muscles tensed.

The decision was Chase's to make.

Trevor's heart pounded in anticipation. They might catch the RMK today, and he wanted to be there to see him taken into custody.

Chase studied him for a long moment. "You ride with Hannah. Given what happened last night, the two of you are probably safest staying with the team."

Trevor relaxed. "Thank you."

"I'll be in the front vehicle with Meadow. Ian and Selena, you take rear position in one vehicle. Hannah, you take the middle position to provide a measure of safety for you two."

They hurried to their respective vehicles and pulled out of the ranch, leaving Isla to man the radio. The main building was still dark as they rolled past it toward the ranch exit.

Hannah seemed focused on the road in front of her. He didn't know how to read her reaction to his inserting himself in the investigation. Even though the suspect had gotten away last night, he felt like they had worked together. Her attitude toward him seemed to have softened.

They followed the lead car on the straight road. It was nearly thirteen miles from the ranch to the campground, which was on the north part of the island. Shortly after passing the sign that indicated Ladyfinger campground, Chase pulled over into a parking lot. The other two vehicles pulled in beside him.

It was still early for the tourists to arrive, but some of the campers may have gotten up to greet the sunrise and hike the trail. There were two other cars in the parking lot.

Chase's voice came on the radio. "The suspect was spotted by one of the campers less than twenty minutes ago out walking Cowgirl. Meadow and I will interview the camper who called this in, as well as others in the area."

Hannah pointed through the windshield. "Ladyfinger campground only has five campsites and it looks like each one was occupied."

"Ian, you and Selena watch the parking lot. If people return to those cars, question them about what they may have seen," said Chase.

From the SUV, Hannah pulled the radio and pressed the talk button. "What do you want me to do?"

"You and Trevor take the hike up to Ladyfinger Point. See if you spot anything."

Her voice went flat. "Roger that."

"Everyone, stay alert. It wasn't that long ago he was spotted. He could still be in the area."

She put the radio back in place. Her lips were pressed together in a tight line.

Trevor leaned toward her. "You're not happy with your assignment?"

"He gave us the least likely place for anything to happen. The farthest away from where the RMK was last spotted."

"He's probably doing that to keep me safe," said Trevor.

They opened their respective car doors and Hannah deployed Captain. The trailhead map indicated the hike was less than a quarter mile.

He'd hiked this trail before, a relaxing walk. They moved past a field filled with sagebrush. In the distance was the Great Salt Lake and a marina that was no longer in use due to the lake shrinking and the water level being so low. He remembered seeing a news story about when it had closed down.

He stopped and turned toward the beach, which was between the trail and the marina. "That must have been where he was spotted down there."

"Yes, but he would have been closer to the campsites to be seen. Weird."

"What's that?"

"He was totally out in the open with the dog, like he wanted to be spotted," said Hannah.

His leg muscles tensed. Had they been lured out here?

The sagebrush gave way to rocks and boulders as they continued their hike. They reached the end of the hike that provided a view of the lake and Egg Island in the distance.

Chase's voice came over the radio. "None of the campers saw our perp head toward the parking lot and leave. That means he must have parked somewhere else. Let me know if you see a car anywhere."

"Roger that," said Hannah. "We are at the end of the trail looking out toward Egg Island. Got a three-sixty view here. I don't see a car anywhere."

Selena reported back that she also did not see any vehicles besides the ones in the parking lot.

Hannah clicked off her radio and continued to study the area. "My parents used to bring me here to spot the birds on Egg Island." She stepped toward a cement pad and peered through the viewfinder.

He'd done the same thing himself on his trips out here. As Hannah swung the viewfinder around, he had a feeling she wasn't looking for birds. "See anything?"

She pulled her eye away from the viewfinder. "I'm just wondering if he didn't park in the lot that connects with the campground and the trail, where did he park?"

Trevor gazed off in the distance. "I suppose he could have parked at the marina."

"Chase will find out exactly where he was spotted. It's a little bit of a walk to get back to the marina." She lifted her head and looked around. "He could have just taken Cowgirl on the shore by the marina. More private and less likely to be seen. I really think he wanted to be spotted."

"So the team would show up?"

Her voice had a chilly quality to it. "Yes."

"You think this is some kind of setup." The RMK would have no way of knowing that Trevor was going out with the team.

"Honestly, I think he takes the dog out when he wants to taunt us." She shook her head. "He's knows it will be reported."

Hannah peered through the viewfinder again. "There is something down there between the marina and the base of this hill." She stepped to one side so he could see. "It looks like a black box."

Trevor looked through the viewfinder. "Where at?"

"Over by that rock outcropping."

He swung the viewfinder. His eye caught something dark and out of focus. He inched it back until what looked like a dark colored box came into focus. "I see it." The object was too far away to discern anything more about it.

Hannah got on her radio to notify Chase of what they had seen. "The box could be connected to the RMK being here."

"Unlikely. Anyone could have left it there," said Chase.

"Permission to check it out," said Hannah. "We can probably hike down to it from here faster than if we had to drive around and walk out from the marina."

"Granted," Chase responded. "If that is what you want to do. We're going to continue with our inquiries down here."

Ian broke in. "One of the owners of the cars has just shown up. I'm going to see if he noticed anything."

The man who arrived at the parking lot must have been walking off trail. Trevor and Hannah had not encountered anyone on their way up.

Hannah signed off. They headed down toward the rocks where the object was. The wind grew stronger the closer they got to the shore, rippling his shirt and hair. Captain's long fur seemed to be flying in all directions.

They drew closer to the rocks, but he still couldn't discern what the cube shaped object was.

"I wish I had binoculars," said Trevor.

They both walked a little faster. The three of them traversed across flat open beach. He had the strange sensation they were being watched. He looked off in the distance. From the empty marina to the rock formations, there were plenty of places someone could be hiding and watching.

Slowly, Trevor began to realize what they were looking at. "That's the kind of crate you put a dog in." There were blankets inside the crate but no sign of any dog.

Hannah pulled her gun. "This could be some kind of trap."

The RMK would have no way of knowing Trevor would be the one to find the crate. Was his intent to take out members of the K-9 team?

They took a few steps toward the crate.

Hannah relaxed her stance, bending her elbows and pointing the gun at the sky. "What is going on here?"

They drew closer. He kneeled to open the crate door as the blanket wiggled. "Well, how about that. Look what we have here."

TEN

Hannah laughed as a furry brown head emerged from beneath the blanket. She holstered her gun.

Trevor had already kneeled down to open the door of the crate. He reached in to grab a cinnamon-colored puppy. "Hello there, little potato." The puppy fit in his hand as he held it to his chest.

"They totally look like Cowgirl," said Hannah. "They must be hers."

There was a water dish and an empty dish that must have contained food. The RMK had not left them here to starve.

The blanket continued to ripple.

Hannah pressed in beside him as he lifted the blanket to reveal three more puppies—one yellow, one dark brown and one a combination of the others' colors. She reached for the yellow bundle.

Captain poked his head between Trevor and Hannah. His fur brushed against her cheek.

Feeling a sense of elation, Hannah pointed the puppy's face toward Captain. "Look what we have here."

Captain sniffed the furry bundle. The dog had always been gentle around anything smaller than him.

"They look well fed." Trevor put the cinnamon puppy back down by his siblings. His hand brushed over the dark brown dog.

"I'd guess they're about eight weeks," she said. "Time enough to be weaned."

Hannah's radio crackled. Chase's voice came across the line. "Hannah, what's going on?"

She put down the puppy and pressed the talk button on her shoulder. "You'll never believe what we found. It looks like the RMK lured us out here so we would find Cowgirl's puppies."

"No kidding. Are they okay?"

"They look like they've been taken care of," she said. "There's four of them."

"We'll be out there as fast as we can." Chase's voice intensified. "Hannah, please be careful. This could still be a trap."

He was right. What had she been thinking? She'd been so caught up in the sweetness of the moment. She stared at the wriggling, grunting fur balls. Her mood shifted as she rose to her feet. There was a stretch of flat land on three sides of them and a lake on the fourth. The rocks would not provide much cover. What better way to get someone's defenses down than for them to find puppies?

It wouldn't be beneath the RMK to use the

puppies as some sort of bait. Her gaze darted toward the marina, where someone might hide, then to the trees in the distance.

"What is this?" After lifting the blanket that covered the floor of the crate, Trevor reached into the cage and pulled out a folded piece of paper. He opened it up and read it. Color drained from his face as his arm went limp.

Her own chest went tight in response to his sudden change of mood. "Trevor? Let me see." She reached down for the piece of paper. A typed note.

For the MCK9 task force. I can't easily elude you and care for them. I'm keeping their mama. I've grown quite fond of Killer. Tell Trevor Gage he'll be dead soon enough.

Hannah felt like a weight had been placed on her lungs. The paper rippled in the breeze. "This will have to be taken in as evidence." She hadn't brought a plastic baggie with her. She put the note in her pocket.

Trevor rose to his feet and stood beside her. "From the way he worded the note, he doesn't realize I'm helping the team out."

If he was watching them now, he would figure it out.

Trevor squared his shoulders and placed a hand

on her arm just above the elbow. "He can't get away with this. We're going to catch him."

While she appreciated his resolve and strength, the content of the note echoed through her brain and chilled her to the bone.

"Let's slip behind these rocks until the rest of the team gets here." She ushered him toward the side of the rocks that faced the lake. The least likely place for the RMK to hide. If he approached from that direction, they'd be able to see him from a long way off. They crouched behind the rocks close enough to the crate to keep an eye on the puppies.

Captain pressed against her on one side and Trevor on the other. She peered over the rim of the stone after pulling her gun. The smell of saltwater permeated the air around her.

The puppies continued to squeak and grunt in the crate.

"Why did he call the dog Killer?" Trevor asked. "I thought her name was Cowgirl."

"That's the name the RMK gave her. He sent pictures of Cowgirl with a collar that says that. We were able to track down the shop in an Idaho town where he purchased that collar."

"In Sagebrush, where Luke Randall was shot?"

Luke had been the RMK's sixth victim. "Yes, I wish the team could have gotten to him before it happened. They were so close to stopping that murder." Still holding her gun, she continued to study the area around her as she spoke.

She shifted her weight. Her knees had grown sore from resting on the sand.

"I feel like he's watching us," said Trevor.

"I get that." Her gaze bounced around to every possible hiding place, looking for any sign of movement or color that seemed out of place.

She was relieved when two patrol vehicles pulled up to the shore. Chase, Selena and Meadow got out, each deploying their K-9s. Chase pointed in two directions. Selena and Meadow both drew their guns and headed to search where Chase had indicated with their dogs heeling beside them.

Hannah and Trevor stood up and made their way toward Chase and Dash.

"Where's Ian?" Hannah asked.

Chase replied, "He stayed with your vehicle and to keep watch."

They led Chase back to where the puppies were.

A faint smile graced his face when he looked down at the puppies climbing all over each other. Chase was a man who didn't wear his feelings on his sleeve, so such a reaction from him was pretty huge.

He kneeled and opened the crate door, then drew out the multicolored puppy. "We'll have to get these little guys back to Elk Valley and have Liana take over their care."

Liana Lightfoot was the team's lead K-9 trainer in Elk Valley. She was set to adopt Cowgirl before the dog had been kidnapped.

"She'll be glad to see them," said Hannah. "Hopefully, we'll get Cowgirl back soon, too."

"Hopefully." Chase stared off into the distance before continuing. "I'll see if I can arrange a chopper to transport these guys."

Hannah could tell that Cowgirl's kidnapping weighed heavily on him.

She stared back down into the crate, trying to inject a hopeful tone into her words. "Looks like they're eating solid food. The blankets will probably have the RMK's scent on them so we can use them for the dogs to track him."

"Yes, all that is good," said Chase. "We'll see if we can get any prints off the crate as well."

Hannah pulled the note from her pocket. Her voice dropped half an octave. "He left this for us to find."

Chase took the note and read it. His expression registered only a minute reaction—a slight parting of his lips, and a subtle deepening of the furrow between his brows. "Our prints will be on this, but we can still send it in for analysis."

Hannah appreciated Chase's steadfastness in the face of such a threatening message.

Selena and Meadow emerged from where they'd been sent to search. They came out to meet the others. Trevor and Chase lifted the crate and carried it across the sand to where the vehicles were parked, then loaded it in the back of Chase's patrol car.

"Selena and Meadow. I want you two to continue to question the campers at the other campgrounds. Hannah, why don't you and Trevor come back to headquarters with me. One of you can ride with me and the other in Selena's patrol car. It's going to be a little cramped. We'll drive you back to your vehicle and you can follow me back to the ranch from there."

They drove back to where Ian and the other patrol car was. Hannah got Captain into his kennel and Trevor sat in the passenger seat.

She turned the key in the ignition and pulled onto the road. She drove toward the ranch behind Chase.

She knew Chase was concerned about Trevor's safety. That was why he wanted them back at headquarters.

The RMK had been on the island for two days, making appearances that he knew would be reported back to them, yet he had not attempted to come after Trevor. The reason for that was now clear. He had been hindered by having to take care of the puppies.

With those four tiny obstacles out of the way, it was just a matter of time before he had Trevor in his crosshairs.

* * *

Trevor couldn't stop thinking about the note the RMK had left. It made the threat on his life that much more real. Sure, the note had chilled him to the bone, but as he stared out the window, he felt something much stronger than fear rising to the surface.

For his dead friends and for the whole town of Elk Valley, he wanted this guy behind bars. The RMK had caused enough pain. Trevor knew he was the only one who could draw the RMK out into the open.

"Do you think he'll try to lure me to a barn, like he did with the other victims? Doesn't it make it that much harder to get at me?"

Hannah didn't respond right away, as though she was weighing what he had said. "The RMK is clever, and he's got to know that we've figured out his patterns. Because he doesn't want to get caught, he might change some of his MO to get to you."

"I agree. Otherwise the only thing I have to do to stay safe is stay out of barns, right." He tried to sound lighthearted.

"He could shoot you and then place your body in a barn." Her tone had grown serious. "My guess is that the barn is a sort of symbol of what the YRC represented."

"I'm the last one left of that friends' group from ten years ago," said Trevor.

"One of the RMK's notes on the recent victims said he was saving the *best for last*. We believe that's you, Trevor. His plan is probably to go after you, and then disappear, making him that much harder to catch."

"All the more reason to stay the course." He found himself praying silently, for courage, as the road clipped by. "The death that bothers me the most is Peter Windham. He wasn't part of the group that pranked Naomi or treated women badly."

Hannah kept her eyes on the road. "The fifth victim, living in Colorado at the time of his death. Someone who wasn't a member of the club wouldn't know that about Peter."

"You're probably right. Maybe Peter was just made guilty by association." He couldn't shake the sharp pain that threaded through his chest. "That is the saddest thing of all."

She nodded.

Hannah turned on the road that led to the ranch and followed Chase's car to the parking area by the community room and bunkhouse. Trevor helped Chase unload the puppies and carry them into the community room while still in the crate.

Isla rose from her desk. She stared into the crate, making oohing sounds. "What a bunch of cuties."

Chase excused himself and stepped outside.

Hannah left the community room and returned

a moment later with a towel. "I had an extra one. I need to pull those blankets for us to use for the dogs to pick up the RMK's scent." Kneeling, she drew out the blankets and put the towel inside for the puppies.

From the window, Trevor could see Chase pace around the building outside with his phone held close to his face.

Holding the water dish, Hannah rose to her feet. Her gaze followed where Trevor was looking out the window at Chase. "He's probably making calls to arrange for the puppies to be transported to Elk Valley."

"Who will take care of them once the puppies get there?"

"Liana Lightfoot, the team's K-9 trainer, will be there to meet them when they arrive," said Hannah. "She'll be overjoyed to see those puppies, I'm sure."

Hannah retreated to the kitchen and returned with a full water dish.

Trevor picked up the cinnamon-colored pup. He was the smallest in the litter, but from watching him interact with his siblings, he appeared to also be the most rambunctious.

Rocco entered from the kitchen. He must have been in the bunkhouse. "What do we have here?"

"The RMK left Cowgirl's puppies for us to find," said Trevor.

Rocco kneeled down and peered into the crate.

"Of course, he'd want to unload these little guys. I imagine they made it that much harder to carry out the final part of his plan." He glanced nervously at Trevor.

Trevor drew the puppy close to him, resting it on his chest. He reminded himself of his resolve to stay on the island to draw out the RMK. The puppy licked the underside of his chin.

Hannah stepped closer to Trevor but looked in Rocco's direction. "How's your head?"

Rocco responded, "Just a bump. I'm cleared for light duty."

Hannah stepped toward the crate and kneeled to pick up an escaping puppy. The other two seemed happy to remain in the crate sleeping.

Still holding the cinnamon-colored puppy, Trevor sat down on the sofa.

Chase stepped into the community room. "Chopper should be here before the day is over to transport the puppies. I'm going to need an officer to accompany them."

"I can go," said Rocco. "I'm supposed to take it easy today, anyway."

"Great," said Chase.

Rocco smiled. "It will give me a chance to say hi to Sadie and Myles." Rocco, who was from Elk Valley, had recently become engaged to a woman who lived there and ran a food truck. Sadie had a three-year-old son, Myles.

Chase put his phone away. "I'm headed back

out to continue searching and questioning. Where are the blankets with the scent?"

Hannah handed one of the blankets to Chase. "We're staying here?"

"For the time being," said Chase. "We'll remain in radio contact. Someone needs to stay behind to watch over Trevor. Rocco can help out, as well, until the chopper comes. I'll make sure at least one officer is back before he leaves with the pups."

Hannah didn't say anything. She simply nodded and placed the puppy she was holding back in the crate. Her disappointment was palpable, though.

With his golden retriever, Dash, following him, Chase excused himself. Trevor could hear his SUV start up outside.

The cinnamon-colored puppy had fallen asleep on Trevor's chest.

"Looks like you are pinned down," said Rocco. "Want me to take him off your hands?"

"Sure," said Trevor.

Rocco reached for the puppy, who grunted and wiggled when he picked him up.

Isla had returned to her computers. Hannah wandered into the kitchen with Captain trailing behind her.

Trevor found Hannah standing at the counter making a sandwich. Captain sat at her feet. "You hungry? We didn't get a chance for breakfast."

"I could eat." He stepped toward the counter and drew out two pieces of bread.

She pushed the packages of cold cuts and sliced cheese toward him. "I'm sorry about you being cut out of the action on account of me," he said.

She took a bite of her sandwich and shrugged. "Sure, I'm frustrated, but I understand. Chase is just trying to keep both of us safe. I respect his judgment."

He squeezed some mustard onto his sandwich. "But it's hard to deal with, all the same?"

"I just thought when this case landed in my backyard that I would be playing a bigger part."

"You are playing an important part. You're protecting me."

"Well, you've pulled my feet out of the fire enough times," she said.

"I think you've handled yourself like a top-notch officer, Hannah."

She lifted her chin as a rich warmth came into her eyes. "Thank you."

It seemed a mutual respect had grown between them. That was progress from where they had started out from.

After they ate, they both wandered into the living room.

Isla looked up from her keyboard. "I'm trying to track down all the part-time and seasonal park employees. I've made a call to the HR person who would have done the hiring. No answer, but I left a message."

"Thanks for doing that, Isla. Maybe that will get us a name to go with the face."

The afternoon dragged on into early evening. Chase and the others all radioed in that the K-9s had not picked up any trail and had not run into anyone who had seen the RMK or Cowgirl since the morning sighting. They were headed home.

It was nearly dinnertime when the chopper landed in a field not too far from the ranch. Trevor helped Hannah and Rocco carry and load the crate.

Rocco got into the chopper with Cocoa after hugging Hannah and shaking Trevor's hand.

Trevor pressed his hand on the crate. "Safe journey, little fellas."

He and Hannah stepped back as the helicopter blade whirled, stirring up dust all around them. They stood close enough that his hand brushed over hers.

As the helicopter gained altitude, she grabbed his hand and squeezed it.

What had her gesture communicated? That they were in this together, willing to fight for each other's lives and safety?

The sound of the chopper grew faint as it became a tiny dot in the expanse of sky.

Trevor stared all around and then back at the edge of the ranch, where the bunkhouse was. It occurred to him that maybe the RMK had not been spotted anywhere on the island since this morning because he had already moved in closer to the ranch and was biding his time, waiting for a vulnerable moment when he could come after his target.

ELEVEN

The team ate a late dinner together while the sky grew dark outside. The heaviness of frustration at the RMK having eluded them seemed palpable. The conversation was mostly about inconsequential things with long silences between comments.

Hannah cleared her throat. Time to address the elephant in the room. "Is there something different we could be doing to draw the RMK out?"

Chase put down his fork as if he was ready to say something.

Trevor interjected. "We could set a trap with bait, namely me."

"I'm not going to put you at more risk," said Chase.

"Seriously, I'll just go stand in a barn somewhere while you guys wait in the shadows." Trevor's words came across as sarcastic.

Ian snorted a laugh.

Chase smiled, as well. He placed his fork on the table. "Appreciate the sentiment, and I feel your frustration, Trevor."

Hannah wiped her mouth with her napkin. "Trevor and I were talking earlier, and we think he might change his MO since he has established a pattern for luring the victims into a barn to shoot them."

"I think that's possible," said Isla. "He's methodical and he's a planner. In order to catch us by surprise, he might try something different."

Chase scooted his chair back, rose and picked up his plate. "We know from the note left on the victims that were killed this past February that he always planned to go after Trevor. That's what he meant by *saving the best for last.*"

It had been clear from the beginning that this case was about revenge. Hannah recalled the contents of the note that had been left on the first two victims. *They got what they deserved. More to come across the Rockies and I'm saving the best for last.*

"What are you saying?" said Meadow.

"I think he sees this K-9 task force as an affront to his careful plan," Chase said. "He thought he was just going to carry out the killings. His anger has spilled over to the task force. That's why he kidnapped Cowgirl, and I believe he's taking delight in evading and taunting us when we are so close to catching him. He's clever and he's adaptable and driven by some deep-seated anger. So, yes, I do think he might change it up, and I wouldn't put it past him to try to target any one of us because he sees us as being in the way."

Hannah let Chase's words sink in but not the fear they had the potential to induce. The team would protect each other. "What's our next step?"

"Meadow, after a couple hours of sleep, you and I will go out on night patrol. We'll get the dog to scent off the blankets that were left in the puppy crate. Selena, you grab a nap, as well, so you can stand guard outside the bunkhouse. Ian, if you're not too tired, why don't you stay close to Trevor along with Hannah?"

After the dishes were done, the three officers left to rest up for an evening of duty.

Isla returned to her computers while Trevor worked on his laptop.

Hannah stood at the window staring at the night sky. The stars were stunning, and they would be even more beautiful if she could go outside and look at them but being exposed like that would be too dangerous.

Antelope Island was known as a great place to star-gaze because of the lack of interference from artificial light due to its remoteness. Memories of last time she and her parents and Jodie had laid on a blanket by the camper to watch the night sky whirled through her mind. The next day, Jodie had been killed.

It marked the end of her childhood and of innocence.

She glanced back at Trevor, who was fully concentrating on his laptop screen. His unruly hair partially covered one eyebrow. What would it be like to star-gaze with Trevor?

Why had that thought popped into her head?

Maybe because there seemed to have been some unspoken agreement between them as they'd watched the helicopter take the puppies away. She'd squeezed his hand to let him know that she was there for him. In terms of keeping each other safe, they had each others' backs. She hoped he understood that she hadn't meant anything more by grabbing his hand.

He had won her trust in that way...at least. That didn't mean her heart was open to anything romantic between them. She'd been hurt one too many times in that department.

Isla piped up. "Hannah, I just got an email from the HR person who hires the seasonal help for the park."

"She's working late."

"It came in several hours ago," said Isla. "I just now had a chance to check it."

Hannah moved across the floor. "What does she say?"

"She gave me three names of possible men that matched the description you gave. They all live in Syracuse. One works in the winter. The other two are spring-summer employees, so they would just be finishing up since it's September. David Weller and Frank Stafford."

"I wonder if they keep their uniforms so they could show up even when they weren't working and not draw attention."

Isla grabbed a piece of paper off her desk and picked up a pen. "She couldn't disclose their addresses, but I can easily match their names to where they live." Her pen whirled across the page. She handed Hannah the piece of paper.

"Thanks, Isla, you're the best." Hannah stared at the three names.

"The first two are the spring-summer employees, probably should look into them first."

Trevor closed his laptop. "I suppose one of the other officers will have to track them down."

That would mean drawing personnel from the RMK case, which might not be possible. "I think maybe we should find out more about them first." She wondered, too, if the culprit would stay away from his home for fear of being caught once they could attach a name to his face.

"I can help you with that, too." Isla turned her attention back to her keyboard. "I'll find if any of them have a police record and do a general search on them to see what pops up. That will help us start building a profile."

"I don't suppose there were photographs of the two men who just finished up their season," said Hannah.

"They don't usually do that for the seasonal help," said Isla.

"It might be helpful to talk to this HR person in the morning. Do you have her name and number?"

Isla grabbed another piece of paper and wrote down the contact information.

Hannah waved the pieces of paper. "I knew once you did your hard work, Isla, we'd make progress." Her mood was elevated by the prospect of being able to identify the man who had come after her.

Shortly after Chase and Meadow left, Trevor and Hannah made the decision to retire. Isla stated that she still had some work to do.

When Hannah glanced at Isla's screen just before she prepared to leave the sitting area, she noticed that she had pulled up the Caring Hearts Adoption Agency website, the agency Isla had been working with to foster Enzo. The look on Isla's face was one of wistful longing.

Isla must have felt Hannah staring. She turned her chair toward where Hannah stood in the doorway.

"Still no word?" Hannah felt her own heart squeeze tight.

"Like looking at the website is going to give me answers." Isla shook her head. "I just wish I could get this thing cleared up and have that little boy in my life."

"I do, too. I've been praying for you. Let me know if there's any way I can help."

Hannah excused herself and headed toward the bunkhouse. Selena had already taken up her position with her K-9, Scout, sitting outside on a chair while Ian took a turn resting.

"Make sure you lock the door behind you," Selena said. "Isla has a key. I checked the room a few minutes ago to make sure it was clear."

Hannah watched as Trevor and Ian headed toward their room, closing the door behind them.

Selena gave a backward glance toward the men's sleeping quarters. "He's all right, Hannah."

"Why are you telling me that?"

Selena shrugged. "Just saying. You seem a little guarded around him and then I see you looking at him like… I don't know, there's some kind of spark between the two of you."

"No, that's not what's going on." She sounded like she was trying to convince herself. "I'm here to do a job and that job is being Trevor's protection."

"If you say so." Selena reached down to stroke her K-9's ear. The Malinois tilted his head in response.

Hannah glanced up at the huge sky and twinkling stars before stepping into the dark room with Captain. She couldn't get away from Selena's probing stare soon enough.

After taking off her gun belt, she removed her

shoes and threw back the covers. She pulled her hair free of the bun it had been in. She fluffed her pillow and lay down, staring at the ceiling. She could hear Captain breathing as he settled down beside her.

"Maybe I do have some feelings for Trevor." She turned on her side, barely able to make out Captain's brown head in the darkness. "What do you think?"

The dog emitted a sympathetic whine.

"Oh, what do you know about love, anyway?" She reached down to touch his head. What did *she* know about it? After her last boyfriend had cheated on her, she had simply closed the door on that possibility. She'd seen the worst side of men in her dating life.

She sighed and closed her eyes, slowly drifting off to sleep. She had the sensation of being pulled through the top of her bed, only it wasn't her bed. Water covered her face. She couldn't breathe. Air, she needed air. Above her was the soft-focus face of the man who had killed Jodie. His hand reached out toward her, slicing through the murky water.

She awoke with a start, her heart racing. The room was dark. Isla's bed was still empty. Captain was lying beside her, snoring.

A knock on the door startled her. Still shaken by the dream, she glanced toward where she'd left her gun.

* * *

"Hannah, it's me." As he lifted his hand from the door, Trevor wasn't sure what had happened. Selena and Scout were no longer posted outside. The chair was empty. The sound of Hannah's screaming had awakened him. Worried that something bad had happened to her, he rushed over to her door.

He heard footsteps and the door swung open. She stood there barefoot but still in her uniform. Her long red hair flowed freely, framing her face.

He breathed a sigh of relief. She was all right. "I heard you scream. What happened?"

"I didn't realize." She stared at the floor. "I had a bad dream." When she looked up at him, her eyes were glazed. "I saw him…in my dream." Her voice faltered. "He was trying to—"

He gathered her into his arms. She was crying and shaking as he stroked her hair and held her close. He hugged her for a long moment, relishing the warmth of her and grateful that he could offer comfort.

She stepped free of the embrace and swiped at her eyes. "Thank you." She shook her head. "The dream just seemed so real." She noticed the empty chair. "Where's Selena?"

"The chair was empty when I left my room to see what was going on with you."

She stepped out onto the concrete pad and

looked in both directions. "She must have seen something."

"We shouldn't be standing outside. I'll wait with you in your room until she comes back. Ian is still asleep."

She nodded and stepped aside. Captain stood wagging his tail. Hannah walked over to the window and peered out. "I wonder what it was that Selena saw."

"I don't know. I didn't hear a gunshot." He stood beside her, seeing nothing but the dark shadows of the trees. "You should probably stay away from the window."

She sat down on the bed, and he settled into the only chair in the room. The embrace had seemed so genuine, he was having a hard time reconciling that with the words he had overheard her say to Selena. That she thought of him as just part of the job. She sent such mixed signals.

The doorknob shook and he realized he hadn't locked it.

The door opened. Isla stood on the threshold. "What's going on?"

Hannah answered. "Selena took off. We think she must have been after someone."

"Oh, my. I hope it was nothing. I hate to think of either of those men being that close."

Yet it was a possibility. The man after Hannah had already tried to lure her out.

"I thought I'd wait here with Hannah until Selena got back," said Trevor.

Isla nodded. "I just came to grab my pajamas and toiletries. I'm ready to call it a night."

The old bunkhouse had no bathroom, so everyone had to use the one bathroom in the community room.

"You stayed up pretty late," said Hannah.

"One thing leads to another. I keep thinking of angles I could be working to move the investigation forward. Since both of our suspects, Ryan and Evan, seem to have fallen off the map, I thought I'd put together a list of people who might know where they are or had seen them. I intend to call them tomorrow if I have any downtime." Isla pulled pajamas, a robe and a bag from her open suitcase on the bed.

"Maybe one of the other team members staying in Salt Lake can assist with that," said Hannah.

"I intend to enlist their help. We still have to track down an address for Ryan. I'd like to put some time into that." Isla pulled pajamas, a robe and a bag from her open suitcase on the bed. She moved toward the door.

Trevor rose to his feet. "I'm going to lock the door behind you. Knock when you come back."

"Got it." Isla reached for the doorknob.

After she left, Trevor rose and pushed the knob in to lock it. Hardly high security.

He sat back down. Their eyes met. He longed to ask what she had meant by saying that she saw being with him as just part of her job, but he was afraid of the answer. Despite how guarded she could be, he was starting to have feelings for her. He couldn't assume that the feelings flowed both ways.

She was a hard person to understand with all the layers of armor she seemed to wear.

Feeling awkward, he got up and peered out the window. Shadows moved by the trees. He took a step back.

"You saw something." She half rose from the bed.

"Stay down." His eyes went to her gun, which she had pulled from the holster and placed on her bedside table.

When he looked back out the window, he saw no more movement.

A pounding at the door caused both of them to jump.

Selena's intense voice boomed through the closed door. "You all right in there, Hannah?"

"Yes," she said.

"Where's Trevor?"

"He's in here with me."

"Oh?" Selena sounded confused.

"When we saw you were gone, we figured something was up. I came in here to make sure she was safe." Tired of talking to the door, Trevor unlocked it.

Dressed in her robe, Isla stood behind Selena.

Hannah spoke over Trevor's shoulder. "Was somebody out there, Selena?"

Trevor turned slightly so Hannah would have a better view.

Scout panted and Selena appeared to be out of breath, as well.

"Scout got all restless and growly, started pulling on the leash. I commanded him to take off. We searched the whole area by the trees."

"There's a lot of wildlife around here," said Trevor.

Selena shook her head. "I don't think that's what it was. Because he's trained to track in all kinds of environments, Scout wouldn't be distracted by other animals, and he was insistent that something was out there."

Hannah came and stood closer to Trevor. He could feel her breath on his neck as she spoke over his shoulder. "At this point, it could have been the RMK or the man who is after me."

Selena put her hands on her hips and let out an audible breath. "I don't think he's coming back tonight. If it was either man, Scout's barking probably scared him away. It wouldn't hurt to have another officer on duty, though. I might wake Ian in a bit."

Trevor stepped out of the way. "Sorry, Isla, didn't mean to keep you waiting."

Selena moved toward her chair. "Why don't you all try to get some sleep?" She commanded Scout to lie down.

"I should probably get some shut-eye, too," said Trevor.

As he left the room, he noticed that Hannah had retreated back toward the nightstand, where she'd pulled out her phone. He wondered whom she would be calling at this time of night but knew that it would have to wait until morning.

He returned to his room. The RMK might have been watching them when they found the puppies. He could have followed them and discovered where they'd set up headquarters. Sleep came slowly. He tossed and turned at the thought that the RMK might be lurking around the ranch watching and waiting for his chance to move in to kill him.

TWELVE

When Hannah woke up, Isla was still asleep. Selena and Scout must have come in sometime in the night, as well. Meadow and Grace were sleeping, too. She grabbed her toiletries and a change of clothes with Captain trailing behind her. She greeted Ian, who sat on the chair outside. Lola was lying at his feet, head up, still alert.

"You couldn't have gotten much sleep."

"I'll get more soon as Chase and Meadow wake up. They came in about two hours ago."

Everyone but her had put in a long night. She felt guilty. She showered and changed. When she came out of the bathroom, Trevor stood by a griddle flipping pancakes. The room smelled like coffee. Scrambled eggs rested in a frying pan on the counter.

"There was a mix in there." He pointed at the cupboard. "Thought I'd try to help out some way."

She grabbed a cup of coffee. "Yeah, I know I feel like I'm not pulling my weight, but I have a plan."

He lifted a pancake with his spatula and transferred it to the plate he'd set out. "Oh?"

She wandered over to the refrigerator and opened it. "I texted Chase last night and asked if I could go talk to the HR woman Isla contacted. Her office is in Syracuse." She spotted some orange juice and pulled it out.

"I assume I'd be going with you?"

"Yes, of course, I still have to look out for your safety so the rest of the officers can concentrate on the investigation. The way I explained it to Chase was that the sooner we can get this man in custody, the sooner I can focus my full energy on helping catch the RMK."

"And what did Chase say?"

"He said it would be all right. I'll call the HR woman and let her know I'm coming in just a bit. I imagine she's not in the office yet."

They ate quickly and cleaned up. Trevor left a note letting the others know there were pancakes in the fridge that could be reheated.

They drove through the park and back over the causeway. Hannah checked the rearview mirror. Only two cars were behind her. Traffic was light this early in the day.

Syracuse was the last town before the island, a place where people picked up supplies or stayed if they wanted something nicer than a camper or tent.

Hannah turned off the main street and drove a few blocks to the park employment office. She unbuckled her seat belt. "Why don't you come with me?"

She didn't notice anyone following them, but she couldn't take any chances.

Leaving Captain in his kennel, Hannah and Trevor stepped into an office where a blond woman wearing pink glasses who looked like she was barely out of her teens sat behind a desk. "Can I help you?"

"I'm Hannah Scott. We're here to see Lydia Strobel."

"You're catching her early. I doubt that she's busy yet." The woman pushed a button on her phone. "Lydia, Hannah Scott and her partner are here."

The assumption the receptionist had made caused Hannah to smile. To the world, she and Trevor came across as two officers working on a case.

Lydia's voice came through the line. "Send them in."

When they entered the office, Lydia Strobel stood by the water cooler filling a water bottle. "Hannah Scott?" Her forehead furrowed when she looked at Trevor.

"Yes, and this is Trevor Gage. He's helping me out."

"I'm not sure what more I can tell you that I didn't already share with Isla," said Lydia.

In Hannah's experience, people were freer with giving information when questioned in person. But what she really hoped for by making the drive was to see if Lydia had pictures of any of the likely suspects.

"I am wondering if you can tell us about David Weller and Frank Stafford."

"I've only been in this position for four years. David has worked seasonally for many years. I'd have to look up his employment record to tell you exactly how many. This is Frank's third year with the park."

"Are both men long-term residents of the area?"

"Yes, I believe so." Lydia took a sip from her water bottle.

Both men must have been responsible enough workers to be hired year after year. "What can you tell me about the personalities of each man?"

"My interaction with both of them was pretty brief. You'd have to talk to some of their co-workers to get a more complete picture."

"I don't suppose you have a photograph of either of the men?"

Lydia took a sip of her water and set it on her desk. "Like I told Isla, we don't usually take headshots for the seasonal workers."

"Maybe something less formal," said Hannah.

"A picnic or a work project a bunch of people were on."

Lydia sat down at her desk and put her hands on the keyboard. "Maybe something on our Facebook page."

It seemed like Isla would have accessed something like that since it was available to the public.

Lydia scrolled through, shaking her head. "Neither David nor Frank do any educational programs. That's mostly what we take pictures of." She looked up and lifted her hands from the keyboard. "Wait." She scooted her chair back and walked over to a file cabinet. "We do take a group picture at the end-of-the-season picnic. I don't have the one from this year yet, but here is the one from last year." She laid a photograph on her desk.

It was a posed photo, three lines of men and women in park uniforms. The front line was kneeling. Hannah scanned the sea of faces.

Lydia stood beside her. "There's Frank Stafford."

She pointed at a man in the middle row.

Hannah shook her head. The features were too sharp. The nose too big. Frank Stafford resembled an eagle.

Lydia continued to scan the picture. "I don't remember if David Weller was in attendance or not."

Hannah's eyes fell on a man in the back row.

He stood in such a way that his face was half-concealed by the person next to him. She recognized the brown curly hair. "That must be David Weller."

"Oh, yes, there he is," said Lydia.

A chill ran down her spine as her heart pounded. The man in the photo was the same man who had come after her. David Weller was Jodie's killer.

Sensing a shift in mood, Trevor stepped closer to Hannah. Her face had drained of color.

"That's him. That's the man." Her voice came out in a hoarse whisper.

Trevor looked at where Hannah was pointing. His face was only partially visible. "Are you sure?"

Hannah nodded. "Can you tell me who David primarily worked with?"

Lydia took the photograph and walked back over to the file cabinet. "I'd have to look up the shift assignments." Her phone rang. She stepped toward her desk. "I can't do that right now but maybe later, and I'll send the information to Isla."

"Thank you, I'd appreciate that." Hannah spoke in a monotone.

Having looked at the face of a murderer, Trevor wondered if she wasn't in a bit of shock.

"Thanks so much. You have been very helpful." Resting his hand on Hannah's upper arm, he guided her toward the door.

Lydia picked up the phone and waved at Trevor and Hannah as they stepped into the reception area.

Once outside, Trevor opened Hannah's car door for her. He climbed into the passenger seat.

"You doing all right?"

She nodded. "I'll be okay in a minute. It's just seeing that man's face kind of put me in a tailspin."

He reached over and rested his palm on her wrist. "Understandable."

She startled when her phone rang. "It's Isla. I'll put it on speakerphone so you can hear it, too." She pressed a button and spoke into the phone. "Yes."

"Hannah, I've got addresses to connect to those names."

"We only need one. David Weller is the guy. Lydia had a photograph."

"That's good news," said Isla. "How are you doing? You sound a little shook up."

"I am. You know, it's been eighteen years since Jodie died. I can't believe that I might finally be free of this cloud that has hung over me for so long."

"Well, that's a good thing." Warmth permeated Isla's voice.

Trevor was grateful that Hannah seemed to

be able to open up more to Isla than to him. It was clear the team members were close and supported each other.

"Yes, it is," said Hannah.

"Anyway, I have David Weller's address. Just wanted to let you know. Chase will probably want to send one of the other officers over there."

"That would be the safest thing. Wait. Is the address clearly a rented apartment? It wouldn't hurt for us to talk to the landlord or manager find out what kind of person David was."

"The address does have a 'half' attached to it so it's probably a basement or an above the garage unit." Isla read off the address while Hannah put it in her phone. "Hannah, maybe you should wait until another officer is available."

Though he understood her urgency in wanting to get the case resolved, Trevor wasn't sure going there was such a good idea.

"It's a weekday. The guy probably had to get to work, or maybe he's hanging out on the island all the time. Besides, Trevor is with me." She gazed in his direction. "We're already over here in Syracuse."

Her vote of confidence in his ability to assist felt good, but he still wasn't sure they should take a chance in going to David's place.

Hannah said goodbye to Isla. She glanced in his direction. "I can tell by the look on your face. You don't like this idea."

Was he that easy to read, or did she just know him so well from all the time they'd been spending together?

"I think talking to the landlord is smart, but what if David is around, he could come after you. Or if he knew you had tracked him to his residence, it might make him flee the state and he'd never be caught."

"We're here in town. The faster we can move this case forward, the sooner I get my life back." She let out a breath and gazed at him. "Please, support me in this."

"Okay, I get it. It's no different than me not wanting to go to a safe house because I feel so much personal responsibility about the murders."

"Why would you feel guilty?" She turned to face him. "In the transcript of your interview you said you really liked Naomi when you asked her to the dance." Her eyes narrowed as she leaned toward him, body language that demanded a clear answer.

At least his conscience was clear about that. "I did like her. I thought she was smart and funny."

Something in her expression relaxed when he gave his answer. "So why do you feel like all the deaths are your fault?"

"If I had spoken up all those years ago, the joke wouldn't have gotten so out of hand," he said. "Even if it's Ryan York who is behind all this, an atmosphere was set in the YRC that led to Seth dumping Shelly. I had influence. I could have changed things and called my friends out."

"I can't argue with you there." A note of irritation threaded through her words.

"Wait. Did you really think I would do something mean like ask a girl out as a joke?"

"I wasn't sure until now. Now that we've talked, I believe you were sincere in asking her to the dance."

"You thought I could do something like that?" Now he understood why there always seemed to be a barrier between them.

She laced her fingers together and stared at them. "I know how Naomi felt. Something similar happened to me in high school. A boy asked him out to a formal dance. I got all dressed up. Mom took me to get my nails done…and then he didn't show. The buzz around the school was that it was on a dare from his friends. I know how mean boys can be."

The anguish in her voice was so intense he wanted to hug her, to comfort her. "I'm sorry that happened to you. That wasn't right."

"It's not just that. My last boyfriend cheated on me. I guess I'm just jaded when it comes to men." She twisted the button on her uniform. "The group you ran with in the YRC didn't come across as stellar examples of manhood."

"Agreed. It wasn't who I really was, and Seth, Brad and Aaron never got a chance to mature and change. It certainly wasn't how my father taught me to treat women, the example he set with my mom. I'm not making excuses, it's just that I was young. I let my peers have too much sway over me."

Warmth came into her eyes as she reached out to touch his hand. "I'm glad we talked about this."

He was, too. He'd seen that vulnerable side of her again. He understood a little better why she was so guarded.

He studied her profile, the subtle spray of freckles across her nose and cheeks. If she was going to be more open from now on, what did that mean for him. Did he deserve to have love in his life when his friends had never gotten that chance?

She turned and put her hands on the steering wheel. "Back to work."

"Yup."

Once the car started rolling, her phone instructed her to turn. She glanced down at it. "I'm only a few blocks from the address. I'm going to circle the block before I stop. Keep your eyes peeled. Any sign of him, and I'll just drive on."

He watched the house numbers. An older woman in a muumuu stood staring at her flower bed at the house where David lived. No sign of David. That didn't mean he wasn't around.

Hannah circled the block and parked around the corner, out of view. "Let's try to catch the landlady while she's in her yard."

They got out. Hannah deployed Captain. Trevor remained close as they turned on the street where David Weller lived.

As they approached the house, he glanced around. Still no sign of David. All the same, he found himself wishing he had his gun.

THIRTEEN

Hannah's heart beat a little faster as they approached the blue house where David lived. All these years, he'd been here probably in this town. Only a short distance away from where she lived in Salt Lake.

The older woman was bent over her flower bed, pulling out weeds. She looked up when they stood at the short fence. The woman eyed Trevor and then Hannah. She hoped her uniform and Captain's K-9 vest would communicate that they were here in an official capacity.

The older woman straightened. "Can I help you?"

"Is this where David Weller lives?"

She massaged her lower back. "David rents a basement from me. He's not here right now."

That made her breathe a little easier. "Is he at work? When will he be back?"

The woman picked up the watering can that rested on the edge of the flower bed. "He hasn't been here for days. He said he was going to take a little vacation before he started back at the job he does once the weather gets cold. What's this about? Has David done something wrong?"

There was no need to fill her in on the details of what was going on. "We just need to talk to him about an ongoing investigation. Did he say where he was going?"

The woman's gray curls bounced as she shook her head. "We don't talk that much."

Hannah assumed that David's *vacation* was spent hiding on the island trying to get access to her. He probably wouldn't return home until he succeeded in his mission.

Trevor stepped forward. "How long has he rented from you?"

"A couple of years."

"What kind of renter is he?"

"He's quiet and keeps to himself. Pays his rent on time."

"Anything unusual about him?"

The woman lifted her head and thought for a moment. "Didn't ever have any family visit him. I guess they moved away years ago. When he talked about his family, it sounded like he didn't like them very much."

"He was estranged from them?"

"Far as I know," said the landlady. "He mentioned having a mom, a dad and a sister. Come to think of it, I never saw him with friends or a girlfriend."

Interesting. Hannah pulled her business card out and handed it over the fence to the woman. "If he does show up, please call us right away."

The woman eyed the card. "You sure he's not in trouble?"

Hannah didn't think the landlady was in any danger from David. "Please just call us."

Hannah turned to walk away when Trevor touched her elbow and bent his head toward the garage, where the door was open. Hannah took a few steps and stretched her neck to see what Trevor was indicating. Inside was a white compact car just like the one that had been following them.

"Ma'am, is that your car in there or David's?"

"Yes, that's my car. I loaned it to David a couple of days ago because he said his car was in the shop, but he got it fixed, I guess."

David must have had the white car at the same time he stole the green Jeep.

"What kind of car did David drive?" Hannah asked.

"Not sure of the model. It was dark blue and had one of those racks on the top for hauling stuff—his mountain bike and his kayak."

More good information. She thanked the woman again before leaving.

Hannah could feel her mood lifting as they

hurried around the block to the car. They had a description of the car David drove. Isla would be able to find out the exact make and model. She was getting a clearer picture of who David Weller was, personality wise.

After loading Captain, she slipped behind the wheel and waited for Trevor to buckle himself in.

"I don't think there's any need to waste precious time on staking out David's place," she said.

"Yeah, it's sounds like he's hiding out on the island," said Trevor.

"It's clear from the attacks that he knows I'm at the ranch. Maybe he's sleeping somewhere during the day and going to the ranch at night since that is when the attack occurred."

"He might change it up, though, now that that hasn't worked. It would be easy enough to blend in the tourist crowd until he saw his opportunity."

"True." As she drove, Hannah thought about the landlady's comment about David not seeming to have any social connections.

She turned onto the causeway, feeling a sense of excitement at the progress they'd made. Once they arrived at the ranch, they found Isla in the community room, along with Rocco.

"You're back," said Hannah.

"Yes, got to see my lovely lady and her little boy. Cooked a nice Italian meal together." Rocco smiled at the memory.

It must be hard to be away from someone you love. Hannah asked, "Did the puppies get settled in?"

Rocco nodded. "Liana made them right at home. Such cute little guys and girls." He rose from the sofa. "Meadow and I are on guard duty, by the way."

"Fine by me," said Hannah. "Chase might want to change up the plan once he hears what we found out."

"What is that?"

Isla piped up. "We have the name of the man after Hannah—David Weller."

"Progress," said Rocco.

"More than that. We tracked down his landlady. He hasn't been home for days."

"That means he's probably on the island twenty-four-seven," said Trevor.

Hannah moved toward Isla's workstation. "We need to find out what make and model of car David is driving."

"That won't take long now that we have a name," said Isla.

Hannah let out a breath and rested her hands on the table. A theory had begun to form in her mind. David's estrangement from family and apparent anti-social behavior was a red flag.

She thought about how the RMK repeated the pattern of shooting his victims in a barn because it was symbolic. David Weller liked to kill by drowning even when he had other easier options. Was the water symbolic? "Can you check on something else for me?"

"What's that?" Isla smoothed her dark brown hair.

"I'm curious if there have been other drownings in the area in the years since Jodie died." As a profile of David Weller emerged, Hannah wondered if David had killed before.

"Give me a little time," said Isla, "and I'll have all that information for you also."

Hannah stepped toward the kitchen with Captain following behind her. Trevor joined her a second later.

She opened the refrigerator. "You want something to drink? Looks like there is some iced tea in here."

"Sure," he said. "Why are you having Isla look up if there were other drownings in the area?"

She handed him a can of iced tea. "As I learn more about David Weller, I'm starting to wonder if we're dealing with a serial killer."

Trevor felt a tightening through his chest at the idea that David Weller may have murdered before. As if he wasn't a sinister enough figure already. "If that's the case, your being able to identify him and connect him to Jodie's murder must have really set him off." He pulled the tab off the iced tea and took a sip. "He's gone all this time without getting caught."

"It's just a theory. We'll see what Isla comes up with."

"Scary though, to think about," said Trevor.

She nodded. "It's part of the job. The clearer the profile we have of David Weller, the easier it will be to catch him."

He saw the fear in her eyes. His knuckles brushed over her cheek. "I'm here for you."

She met his gaze. "I appreciate that." Her voice was soft and lilting.

Rocco poked his head into the kitchen. "Isla found something."

They stepped away from each other, though Rocco had probably noticed how close they'd been standing to each other. They both entered the seating area. Hannah took a seat beside Isla while Trevor and Rocco peered over their shoulders at the screen Isla was looking at.

"First, I looked up to see if David Weller had ever had any criminal charges brought against him."

Hannah shifted in her seat. "Anything?"

"No, not so much as a parking ticket, no restraining orders, nothing."

Trevor relaxed a little and took in a deep breath. Maybe that was a good sign.

Isla fingers flew across the keyboard. "Then I looked up to see if there were any other drownings, either accidents or homicides, in this area. There was one a few years after Jodie died." Isla brought up a page of a Syracuse newspaper.

Trevor read the headline. "She died in a pool in a Syracuse hotel." The article featured a photograph of a woman who was maybe in her late forties.

Hannah leaned forward, scanning the article. "Was it an accident?"

"When I pulled up the coroner's report, the cause of death was listed as inconclusive. She did have some alcohol in her system, but there was also some bruising on her wrists and neck."

Trevor looked closer at the article. "She was traveling by herself."

Isla typed some more. "Then we have this just last year. A man drowned in one of the freshwater springs here on the island. They do think it was a homicide. Those streams are not that deep. The man was hit on the back of the head. They never caught the guy who did it."

Trevor stared at the photo of the man. Probably about the same age as the woman.

"Any connection between any of the victims including Jodie?" said Hannah.

"None that I could find. The crimes seem fairly random."

"Man, woman and child," said Trevor. "Like a family."

Isla turned in her chair and looked at him. "Exactly." Her eyes lit up. She swung back around and typed some more. "I wonder."

"What are you looking up?"

"Trying to find out about David Weller's family. Give me a minute. This might require some digging."

"The landlady said that she thought they had moved away from here," said Hannah.

Trevor and Rocco both stepped away. He wandered over to where Cocoa sat at attention, then brushed his hand over the dog's head and peered out the window that faced the gravel lot where the cars were parked. Outside, Chase had just pulled up in his vehicle, an expression of concentration on his face as he opened the door so Dash could dismount.

Chase entered the room. His face had a slackness that suggested fatigue.

Rocco, Hannah and Trevor all looked in his direction.

"Any developments?" asked Rocco.

Despite his obvious weariness, Chase squared his shoulders. "Actually, we got a little bit of a lead. The RMK was spotted at White Rock campground during the day yesterday. When we went to the campsite the witness had indicated, no one was there. That means he's moving around from campground to campground."

"Maybe sleeping during the day," suggested Hannah.

Chase shifted his weight and ran his hands through his brown hair. "Yes, and then taking off at night while Cowgirl is sleeping."

"Probably to come watch the ranch to wait for his chance to get at Trevor," said Hannah.

"We don't know that for sure. Trevor hasn't been attacked while at the ranch," said Chase. "Even if he eluded us again, we gained some information from the witness. The RMK is in one of those vans that has a bed inside. He can conceal Cowgirl in there. No windows in the back. The witness thought it referenced a rental company on the side. He couldn't remember the name."

"We've found out quite a bit about the man who came after me," said Hannah. She filled him in on all they had learned about their suspect but didn't share her serial killer theory.

"That is some good police work," said Chase. "I just came back for some food and to grab a little sleep. We'll continue to search the island for both men."

So far, it had only been David Weller who had attacked them at the ranch. The RMK had yet to make a move. If the RMK had been watching when they found the puppies, he would know that Trevor was assisting them. They still needed solid evidence the RMK had figured out that they were using the ranch as their headquarters. Unfortunately, that evidence might come in the form of an attempt on Trevor's life.

Isla rose from her chair and stretched. "I have something to show you all that is quite interesting."

FOURTEEN

Hannah and the others hurried over to where Isla had settled back down in her seat.

"It took a little digging, but I found a picture of David Weller and his family. The dad was given some kind of award for a civic club he belonged to. The family had their picture taken together for the paper." She brought up a photograph. A younger David Weller with his mom, dad and sister. David looked to be in his teens. To a degree, Mom and Dad resembled the other two victims. Similar haircuts and a sort of suburban middle-class style. The round innocent face of David's sister stared out from the old photo.

Hannah's breath caught in her throat as she bit her lower lip. Just as with the parents, the resemblance was not exact, but David's sister looked to be about the same age as Jodie when she died.

Hannah put her hand over her mouth. "It's like he killed his family."

"Exactly," said Isla. "Like you said Hannah,

the actual family is alive and well and no longer living in this area. I have one more tidbit for you."

"Go ahead," said Trevor.

"Out of curiosity, I wondered what David did for a living when he wasn't working at the park. He's a lifeguard at the indoor city pool and he teaches classes at a private school."

"We're talking about a guy who feels very comfortable in the water." Hannah recalled that the first time she'd encountered David he had shown up in a boat.

"Yes, maybe he doesn't have a lot of confidence in other aspects of his life, but he feels like he's in control when he's in water. It's not that he had trauma connected to being drowned," said Isla. "It's that he feels like the strong one in the water."

Hannah rubbed her goose-pimpled arms. The new information made her thoughts run in different directions all at once.

Chase excused himself to go get some food.

Hannah sat down on the couch. Trevor and Rocco wandered away from the computers, as well. If the deaths were connected, she understood now why David wanted her dead. He'd done his killings and then his work allowed him to return to the spot where the first one, Jodie, had happened. He could have continued for years without anyone connecting the deaths. "Isla, did any witnesses come forward for the other two deaths?"

"Not that I could find. I read the coroners' reports and the initial police investigations, which both went cold," said Isla.

The deaths would have remained unsolved if she hadn't recognized David at the beach days ago. She was the only one who could put him in jail.

Chase returned with a plate of food. "Isla, all this information is interesting in understanding who we're after from a behavioral and psychological standpoint. We know why he did what he did, but none of it helps us catch him."

Isla lifted a finger in the air. "Touché. My research has not been all focused on the forensic psychology of it all. I also was able to find out exactly what kind of car he drives through DMV records. I can pull up a picture of a similar model."

"The one David drove had a rack on it for bicycles and other outdoor equipment," said Trevor.

Chase took a bite of the hot dog he'd prepared. "License-plate number?"

"Yup," said Isla.

"That is solid. We can put out the information to the park police. We should be able to track him down that much faster," said Chase.

"I'll get the notice out, along with the photo of a similar model," said Isla.

"Maybe we'll have him in custody before the

day is over," said Hannah. The possibility lifted her spirits.

Chase sat down at the table to finish his hot dog. Hannah took a seat opposite him. "Chase, we think both the RMK and David Weller may be watching the ranch waiting for their chance. I don't know that either Trevor or I are any safer staying confined here and it requires another officer to be pulled off the search to provide extra protection."

Chase held up a hand. "I know what you are going to ask. The attack on you occurred at night. Even the guy Selena saw tried to move in under the cover of darkness. That's the most dangerous time."

"You still want us to stay here during the day?"

Chase wiped crumbs off his fingers. "What we've got to do is beef up security at night for the two of you and to maybe flush the culprits out. We still need solid evidence that the RMK has zeroed in on the ranch."

Captain sauntered over to stand beside Hannah's chair. "Okay, we'll stay here." She reached down to pet him.

Isla pulled off her headset. "I just got a call. The RMK was spotted over by the Island Buffalo Grill without Cowgirl."

"I'm on it," said Chase, rising from his chair. "Dispatch Ian, Selena and Meadow. Whoever is close." Chase hurried out the door. "Maybe we can get him this time."

"I'll stay put," said Rocco.

Hannah sat down beside Trevor, who reached over and patted her hand. "I know it's hard to be out of commission like this."

She appreciated his show of support. The warmth of his touch lingered even after he pulled his hand away. She was a part of this team, and she still could make a contribution. "We should see what kind of food is in that kitchen. Maybe we can prepare something other than junk food for when the rest of the team shows up."

"Sounds good. I'll give you a hand."

Rocco paced the floor, looking out each window before stepping outside, probably to patrol the exterior each of the buildings with Cocoa.

Hannah and Trevor retreated to the kitchen. She inspected what was in the fridge and the freezer. "Looks like there is stuff for a roast in here." She put a bag of carrots on the counter.

Isla stood in the doorway. "I just got a call. David's vehicle was spotted." Her voice held an edginess to it.

Hannah turned to face her. "That's good news. Where at?"

Isla's jawline grew tight as she rubbed her upper arm nervously. "It's here on the ranch, over by where the horses are kept that people can rent for trail rides."

Hannah knew what she had to do. There was no time to seek Chase's permission. "We can get to him faster than anyone. The others are on the way to where the RMK was sighted." She raced toward the door. When she got outside, she didn't see Rocco anywhere. She had hoped for some backup.

She clicked on her radio. "Rocco, where are you?"

"I saw suspicious movement in the trees and had to check it out."

Trevor had followed her outside. "I'm going with you."

She didn't want to go into this alone and it would take precious minutes for Rocco to come back. She spoke into her radio. "Isla will fill you in when you get back." She turned toward Trevor. "Hop in."

Captain was already waiting by the back door of the SUV.

It would be a short drive to get over to the horse stables. She prayed they would be able to take David Weller into custody.

They arrived at the horse-rental area within minutes. Somehow, Trevor had a feeling David Weller hadn't come here to ride a horse for the afternoon. Maybe he figured he'd park his car in an out-of-the-way place, walk over to the bunk-house and look for a chance to get at Hannah.

He didn't see David's car anywhere.

Four people leaned on the fence watching the horses in the corral. Two of them were young children.

A man in a park police uniform walked toward the patrol vehicle as they got out.

Hannah held out her hand. "Are you the officer who phoned this in?"

The man nodded. "Just noticed it a few minutes ago." He pointed. "It's on the other side of that barn."

"Did you see the man who was in the car?"

"No. It was unoccupied when I walked over to it." The man turned slightly. "I have met David Weller, though."

"What can you tell me about him?"

"Bit of an odd duck. Quiet in an eerie way. Guess he's a hard worker. Shows up on time, mostly does cleanup."

Hannah thanked the man and asked him to stay close in case they needed backup. As he walked away, she glanced around. "I think we should park my patrol vehicle out of sight. And then watch the car to see if he comes back."

They hurried back to the SUV. Hannah found a hiding spot for the patrol vehicle behind a copse of trees. After deploying Captain, they walked the short distance past the corral. Several people rode horses toward the trailhead.

David's car was parked off to the side of the

building where people paid for their rentals. A red station wagon was beside it. Hannah circled the vehicle and peered in the windows.

They both studied the area around them. "It would be a little bit of a walk to get over to the bunkhouse," said Trevor.

Hannah turned from side to side as if she was thinking about something. "David is employed by the park service. Even if he's not working right now, he might be in touch with other employees. Maybe he receives emails. That notice about his car went out to all park-service employees."

"You think he got info that might have tipped him off?"

"Could be he didn't want to have the car spotted too close to the bunkhouse," said Hannah. "And maybe word got back to him and he abandoned the car."

They stepped inside the building.

A short woman with black spiky hair, probably in her early twenties, stood behind the counter. "Did you folks want to go on a trail ride?"

"We're here on police business. Is that your red station wagon outside?"

"Yes." She eyed them suspiciously as she took a step back. "What is this about?"

"Did you see the man who parked the car next to yours?"

"That's employee parking. I didn't realize there was another car there." The woman came from around the counter and stared out the window. "He or she must have parked there after I got here."

"And when was that?"

"I started my shift fifteen minutes ago."

That meant they weren't too far behind David. Trevor and Hannah stepped outside.

Hannah pressed the button on her radio. "Rocco, how are things there?"

"Quiet. What's going on with you? Any sign of David?"

"Just his car. I think we'll stake out the area and see if he comes back to it."

"You want me to come help?"

"Stay put. He might be headed your way."

"Ten-four. I'll run a patrol of the area."

"Stay in touch," she said.

Hannah turned to face Trevor. "Why don't we find a hiding spot? We'll give it a half hour."

They circled the building, not finding any place that provided a view of the car but would keep them concealed.

"Let's just watch from inside the building. We can see the car from that window."

They returned to the building, taking up a place on either side of the window. While they waited and watched, a couple came in to pay for the horseback ride. They eyed Hannah and Trevor before turning toward the woman behind the counter.

"When is the next guided horseback ride?" The man stretched his arm around the woman's back and squeezed her shoulder. She peered up at him. Two people who were clearly in love.

Hannah moved her attention away from the window, toward the couple. Trevor couldn't quite read the look on her face. When he caught her staring, though, her expression changed. Had she given up on the possibility of love for herself, yet longed for it?

The spiky-haired woman said, "The next group leaves in half an hour."

Hannah's radio crackled and she pressed the talk button. "What's up, Rocco?" She walked toward the door.

Trevor followed her outside. He stepped closer to her so he could hear both sides of the conversation.

Rocco's voice came across the line. "Two things. There was a man on a mountain bike pedaling by here real slow, over by the road."

Her voice faltered a bit. "Did it look like David?"

"Couldn't tell for sure. He had a helmet on, and he was far enough away so I didn't have a clear view of his face. I just happened to be on the back side of the bunkhouse that faces that road. He seemed to be watching the bunkhouse awful close, and he zoomed off when I spotted him."

Hannah didn't answer right away. With her

head still bent toward the radio, she leaned a little closer to Trevor. "You said two things."

"Yes—Isla heard from the rest of the team. The call was a false alarm. When they got there, they spotted a man who looked like the RMK. He said a man paid him to wear the sunglasses and baseball hat and show up in that area."

"A decoy," said Hannah.

"The rest of the team is headed back here. Chase thinks the RMK might be somewhere on the grounds."

Tension threaded through Hannah's voice. "The RMK wanted most of the team to be called away so Trevor would be vulnerable."

Trevor tensed, pressing his teeth together. "He's close," he whispered under his breath.

Hannah glanced up at him and then spoke into the radio. "We're headed back to the bunkhouse. We'll get there as fast as we can." She lifted her finger off the talk button.

Both of them stared out at the ranch. Plenty of people wandered through the farm.

"Let's get back to your vehicle." Trevor guided Hannah to where they had hidden the car.

Hannah was reaching to open the back door when Captain barked and stared out toward one of the other buildings. "What is it, boy?"

Trevor searched the area that had alarmed Captain, not seeing anyone who looked like the RMK.

Hannah shot a nervous glance at Trevor. "He might just be picking up on our fear."

She got Captain loaded into the kennel.

Trevor grabbed his seat belt and secured it as she pulled out from behind the trees and veered toward the dirt road that led back to the bunkhouse. "Do you think David will go back to his car or has he ditched it permanently?"

"I'm not sure. He can't get around much without it. He may have a boat stashed somewhere. That first day when I saw him, he was in a small motorboat. Even that would limit where he could go. We need to have somebody watching that car all the same if there is even a small chance that he will return there."

"It just can't be you and me doing it, given what we think the RMK is up to?" said Trevor.

"If the RMK is lurking around here, you can't be out in the open," she said.

She took the winding dirt road that led to the community room with the bunkhouse behind it.

When they arrived, Rocco's patrol vehicle was the only one parked outside. They got out. Trevor could see tourists circling around some of the buildings that were closer to the community room, as well as people walking through the fields where the freshwater stream and trails were.

Chase and the rest of the team hadn't made it

back yet. As they walked toward the door, Trevor noticed that Hannah had unclipped that strap that held her gun in place.

She sensed their vulnerability, too.

FIFTEEN

Even once she and Trevor were safe inside the community room, Hannah found no relief from the tension that snaked around her torso and made it hard to breathe. With two killers probably close by, it felt like they were under siege.

Rocco stood up from the couch. "Glad you made it back. Hannah, if you want to stay inside with Trevor, Cocoa and I will patrol the exterior of the building."

Hannah nodded. "We need to get someone watching David's car as soon as possible."

"I don't think it would be a good idea for me to leave the premises just yet." Rocco cupped his hand on Hannah's shoulder. "For now, I need to stay close to you and Trevor."

Isla emerged from the kitchen. "I just made a fresh pot of coffee if you guys want some. Chase and the rest of the team should be here soon."

Trevor moved toward the kitchen. "I'll get you a cup."

Rocco exited through the front door. Standing

to the side, Hannah watched from the window as Cocoa heeled dutifully beside Rocco.

Trevor held a steaming mug out to her. She took the cup. "You might want to stay away from the window." Both men had guns and could take a shot from a hiding place.

"I'd say the same to you," said Trevor.

She took a tiny step back. "I'm being careful. I have to watch." After checking out of the other two windows in the community room and then going into the kitchen to look through the window that provided a view of the bunkhouse, Hannah was satisfied that neither man was approaching the house. She caught a glimpse of Rocco as he headed through the field toward the trees. He was vulnerable out there alone. When were Chase and the rest of the team going to get back?

She took a drink of her coffee, enjoying the warm richness of the liquid and the intense aroma. Then she walked back into the seating area. Isla was busy at her computers, and Trevor sat on a couch. After taking a sip of coffee, he put down his cup and rocked back and forth before rising to his feet. He was as restless as she was.

Captain rested on the floor with his head up looking around. He thumped his tail when he saw Hannah. She bent down to pet him and ran her fingers through his thick fur.

A distant pop caused Hannah to fall to the floor. "That was a gunshot. Get down."

Isla had already dropped to the floor.

After commanding Captain to follow, Hannah crab-crawled to the front door and burst outside. She pressed close to the building and peered out, not seeing Rocco anywhere.

Trevor appeared in the doorway and then moved against the wall close to Captain.

"You need to stay inside," he said.

"So do you. I can't leave my colleague out there alone." She pressed the talk button on her radio. "Rocco, come in. Where are you?"

No response.

She dared not try a second time. The sound of the radio might give Rocco away if he was still in the shooter's crosshairs. He and Cocoa could just be laying low and trying to be quiet to avoid being shot at again. Or, he might already be shot and bleeding out.

The notion paralyzed her for a moment. What should she do?

She rationalized that if he had been shot, it seemed as though his K-9 would have raised the alarm with barking. Rocco must be okay but unable to respond.

"I have to go out there," said Hannah. "I can't leave him stranded. He might be pinned down."

"Then I'm going with you," said Trevor.

Isla peeked around the doorway while she used

the wall to block most of her body. "Which direction do you think the shot came from?"

Hannah shook her head. "I'm guessing this side of the house and more toward the trees." That's where the potential hiding places were, anyway.

"I'll stay close to the main radio," said Isla.

With Trevor following her, Hannah and Captain hurried in the general direction she thought the shot had come from.

Rocco's voice came across the line in a low whisper. "I think I lost him."

Hannah scanned the trees, catching a flash of movement. "I think I see him. I'm on it."

"Which way?"

"Not sure. He disappeared." Hannah gasped for breath as she ran and tried to talk at the same time.

She hurried toward the trees, where she'd seen a flash of neon yellow that contrasted with the gold-, red-and rust-colored leaves that hung on the trees.

Wind made the dry leaves rattle as she and Trevor entered the trees.

"Over there." Trevor sprinted ahead of her.

She moved to catch up.

They came to a yellow mountain bike propped against a tree. Both of them slowed their pace, then stopped abruptly. Captain was on full alert.

The first gunshot came so close to Hannah's head that her ears rang from the intensity of it.

They both fell to the ground as the second shot zinged over them. Hannah pulled her gun, took aim and fired a shot.

Rocco's voice came across the radio. "I heard that. On my way."

Hannah wasn't sure which way Rocco would be coming from. "Approach with caution."

More shots were fired. They were driven deeper into the trees. They no longer had a clear view of the bicycle.

With her gun lifted, she watched the foliage. She heard the breaking of branches off to the side but could not risk hitting Rocco. Her heart pounded as she watched and waited to see some sign of who was coming toward them.

Rocco and Cocoa emerged through the thick underbrush.

Hannah pointed. "He's over that way."

The three of them rushed in the direction they had just retreated from. When they arrived in the open area where the bike had been, she saw that it was gone.

"He's must be headed toward that dirt road," said Trevor.

"I'm going back to get my vehicle to see if I can head him off via the road." Rocco turned back around.

"Great, we'll pursue on foot," said Hannah.

With Captain by her side, she and Trevor moved toward where the trees opened up to a flat grassy area. Beyond that was the dirt road. There was no sign of David Weller or his bike. With her gun still drawn, she ran toward some brush that provided a degree of cover.

In one direction, the curved road was partially concealed by a rock formation. In the other direction, the road was straight. She could see the outskirts of the ranch in the distance.

When no shots were fired in their vicinity, she stepped out and moved toward the road. Mountain-bike tracks had left an impression in the road where it was soft, but they soon faded on the harder packed dirt.

Trevor pointed toward where the road curved. "He must have gone that way."

Rocco's car came into view on the part of the road that was straight. He slowed his vehicle as he approached. Then stopped with the engine still running while he rolled down the window and leaned out. "Any sign of him?"

"We think he went that way." She pointed.

"I should be able to catch him." He closed the window as the SUV rolled forward and sped away.

Rocco had rounded the curve by the rocks before Hannah could suggest he needed backup. The three of them and two K-9s would have been cramped in the car, anyway. The kennel took up most of the back seat. For sure, she could not leave Trevor unguarded.

"I guess we head back." They trudged up the road, toward the ranch.

After nearly five minutes, Rocco's voice came across the radio. "He's not here. I should have caught up with him if he stayed on this road."

"Where could he have gone?"

"I passed a sign for a trailhead a ways back."

Hannah looked off in the distance, where a trail led up a rocky hill. She could just make out a bicycle as the sun glinted off the metal. The neon yellow of the rider's clothes was also evident. The rider remained still at the peak looking in their direction, then disappeared over the other side. How menacing.

Hannah still had her hand on the radio. "I think we lost him."

Disappointment permeated Rocco's voice as it came through the radio. "I'll get turned around and come so you guys can use my patrol vehicle. Neither you nor Trevor should be out in the open for too long, but we can't all fit in the vehicle."

Hannah let go of the radio. They were standing out in the open, easy targets for a man with a gun, if he was close. They still didn't know where the RMK was.

Trevor reached for her hand and squeezed it. "He can't get far on just a bicycle."

The muscles around her mouth tightened. "Yeah, but he knows this island and all the possible hiding places. He's managed to evade us so far."

"He can't hide forever," said Trevor.

Clearly shaken, she pressed her face into her palm. "We're so close to catching him."

His heart squeezed tight over how distressed she was. "We'll get him. You have a great team of officers backing you up."

She lifted her head, revealing the tears forming in her eyes. "Sometimes it feels like this will never end."

He wrapped his arms around her and drew her close. "We'll do this together."

She turned her face up to look into his eyes. He longed to comfort her and ease the pain he saw on her face.

"I know I have to keep believing that and not lose hope." Green eyes stared at him, searching. Her gaze held a magnetic pull he could not resist.

He bent his head and kissed her. She seemed to melt against him as her hand rested on his chest.

His heart pounded as he breathed in the floral scent of perfume.

The sound of an approaching car cut the kiss short. They both stepped away from each other at the same time.

Heat rose up his neck. He looked toward where Rocco's patrol car had come into view. He stopped the car, got out and deployed Cocoa.

"We'll walk back," he said, handing Hannah the keys.

Once they were settled in the patrol car, an awkward silence surrounded them. What had that kiss even been about? Had he just caught her at a vulnerable moment or was she opening her heart to him?

He wasn't even sure of his own feelings. He had so wanted to comfort her.

He cleared his throat.

She started talking before he could say anything. Her words had a nervous rapid-fire quality to them. "I just hope Chase understands why I left the community room. I don't know why those guys are taking so long in getting back, anyway…" She glanced in his direction and then continued to talk about the case.

Okay, so the kiss had made her nervous or confused her.

Hannah drove on the dirt road and turned into the ranch. In order to get back to the bunkhouse, they had to go past the busier parts of the ranch. Trevor found himself scanning the crowds and clusters of people, looking for a blond man in sunglasses and a hat. He doubted Cowgirl would be with the RMK if he was getting ready to make a move.

When they arrived at the community room, there were two other patrol vehicles parked in the dirt lot. Chase and the others were back.

Inside, Chase and Ian were sitting at the table sipping coffee.

Chase looked up as they entered and addressed his comments to Hannah. "Isla filled me in on the excitement. I've sent Selena to watch David Weller's vehicle. It was ill-advised for you to leave the protection of the community room, but I understand why you did it."

"I couldn't leave Rocco stranded out there while he was being shot at."

"I get that. Where is he, anyway?"

"He's walking." Trevor felt the need to defend Hannah. "We both needed the protection of a vehicle."

"I am trying to make smart choices." Hannah pulled a strand of red hair behind her ear. "But I feel an obligation to help out as much as I possibly can."

"I know that." Chase put his coffee mug down. "All the same, as much as possible stay close to the community room and to Trevor. He's in just as much danger as you are."

Ian rose to his feet and picked up his cup. "I'm going to get some sleep."

Chase said, "We have the RMK's scent on the blankets from the puppies. Grace, Meadow's dog, is trained to track. If the RMK is at the ranch, maybe she can find him."

Trevor tugged on Hannah's sleeve. "We were

in the process of trying to get that roast in the oven when we were interrupted."

Maybe if they were alone and working on something together, they both would relax, and they could talk about the kiss.

Hannah followed him into the kitchen. She searched the cupboards until she found a large roasting pan. "How about I cut potatoes while you brown the meat?"

"Sounds good." He moved toward the refrigerator and took out the roast.

They both worked in their respective areas. Trevor found a frying pan and oil. He removed the meat from the packaging, enjoying the sizzle when he placed it in the hot oil.

Hannah cut potatoes with an intense energy.

Trevor placed the browned meat in the roasting pan. "Now what?"

She turned back toward the counter, grabbing a cutting board. "I think I saw an onion in the produce bin."

He took the cutting board, retrieved the onion and a knife, then stood beside her at the counter while she continued to work on the potatoes.

Her shoulder brushed against his sending an electric charge through him. "Listen, about that kiss. I didn't mean to be forward. I don't know where I stand with you."

She sliced through the potatoes, making rapid pounding noises on the cutting board. She turned toward him. "It's all right. Maybe we both just got caught up in the moment."

It felt like a rock had dropped in his stomach as he tried to sort through his confused feelings. "Sure. That must have been it."

She turned back toward her task. She'd made it clear she didn't want him reading anything into the kiss.

They finished putting the roast together without any further conversation other than exchanges about the logistics of the cooking.

The day wore on. Trevor spent his time trying to focus on the work he could do on his laptop or phone. When Ian woke up, Chase sent him out to continue to search the ranch. Selena radioed that there still was no sign of David Weller returning to his car.

While the room filled with the aroma of the roast cooking, Hannah retrieved a book from her patrol car and sat down on the opposite end of the couch from Trevor to read.

She offered him a quick nervous smile before turning her attention to her book. Even that brought back the memory of how right it had felt to hold her and kiss her.

The team regrouped with all but Rocco who took over the stakeout on the car, so Selena could have a break. Ian as well was still searching the ranch. They ate dinner together after Chase said grace.

"I'll stand guard outside the bunkhouse. Meadow and Selena, I'd like you two to continue to search the grounds at night. Your K-9s have the best training for finding the RMK. Take a power nap if you need one. If David Weller doesn't show up for his car under the cover of darkness, he's probably not going to come back to it. We won't continue the stakeout on the car. I can't waste precious personnel if it's proving to be a dead end."

"There must be something I can do?" said Hannah.

Chase pushed his chair back from the table. "I can't risk your safety, Hannah. If David Weller only has a bike for transportation, he's not going to go far from the ranch."

"I understand," she said.

Hannah's disappointment was palpable to Trevor. "Hannah thought David might have access to a boat. He was in one the first time he came after her. He could be getting around that way."

"Could be. That limits him, too."

Isla piped up. "Hannah, I'll pull up some pictures of boats and you can tell me which one best matches the one you saw."

"The marina's not in use," said Chase. "Where would he dock it?"

"It was a small craft. There are hundreds of little inlets around the lake where he could pull it up on shore. I know most of them from having come here as a kid," said Hannah.

"Would you be able to point them out on a map?"

Hannah shook her head. "I'd have to show them to you in person."

"Maybe Hannah and I and another officer could check the sights out in daylight," suggested Trevor.

"Maybe. We'll see what tonight yields." Chase rose holding his plate. "I'll be patrolling outside with Dash. Hannah, you stay here with Trevor."

Trevor spent the rest of the night finishing the work on his laptop.

After about an hour, Hannah put down the book she'd been reading and rose from the sofa. "I finished this. I'm going to grab my Bible from my bag." I'll just be a minute."

Isla rose from the sofa, where she'd been watching something on her phone with headphones. "I think I'm going out for a walk to get some air. Lock the door behind me."

"Can do," said Trevor.

After Isla left, Trevor tapped the keys on his laptop as he assessed the profit margins on a cattle ranch that was considering expanding into other livestock and updating some equipment.

Trevor massaged his temples. His eyes hurt from staring at a computer screen. Hannah should have been back by now.

The radio on Isla's desk fizzled with static and then a voice came through the line. "Isla, Chase…are you there?" The voice was Selena's.

Why wasn't Chase picking up?

Trevor walked over to Isla's workstation. He pushed the talk button. "Selena, it's Trevor. Isla just stepped out. Not sure what is up with Chase."

"We spotted a guy slinking around the grounds. Tall, like the RMK, but we couldn't get a good look at him. He could be headed your way."

"Thanks. I'll go let Chase know."

Trevor hurried into the kitchen. Before opening the back door, he peered out the window that provided a partial view of the bunkhouse.

Chase was lying on the ground outside the bunkhouse. The door that led to the men's sleeping area had been flung wide open. Dash was nowhere in sight.

Heart pounding against his rib cage, Trevor's first thought was concern for Hannah's safety.

He ran toward the back door when the knob shook. Isla or Hannah would have spoken up and Isla probably would have come to the front door.

Someone was trying to breach the locked door. He froze, watching the shaking doorknob.

He pulled himself from his paralysis. He needed to get his phone in the other room.

Just as he turned to go, a gunshot exploded outside. The intruder was trying to shoot the door open.

SIXTEEN

The blast of a gunshot caused Hannah to jump. She'd taken way too much time looking for her Bible when she should have stayed with Trevor. She grabbed her firearm from the side table. Captain barked when they stepped outside.

She took in the scene. Chase was lying on the ground. Where was Dash? She checked for a pulse. Alive but unconscious. No sign of a gunshot wound.

Inside her room, she could hear her phone ringing. No time to go back to get it. She'd left her utility belt behind, as well.

It sounded like the shot had come from outside the community room. She ran around the corner. A man stood by the back door, covered in shadows.

"Police—put your hands up."

The man turned around, fired a shot in her direction and took off running. The shot had gone wild. Her feet pounded the hard earth as she followed the man into the darkness.

The man's baseball hat had fallen to the ground as he headed toward a cluster of buildings and sheds. In the moonlight, she saw blond hair... the RMK. As she drew closer to the buildings, she lost sight of him. She slowed down, scanning the areas around the buildings, listening for any sound that might be out of place. Her eyes had not yet adjusted to the darkness when she reached an open-sided shed. She aimed her gun at the interior of the structure as her eyes scanned for movement. Stillness answered back.

Her heartbeat thrummed in her ears. She swallowed to produce some moisture in her mouth. She gripped the gun with both hands, ready to take a shot.

Backup would be nice, but her radio was back in her room.

Captain brushed against her leg, reminding her that she was not alone in this fight.

Satisfied the perp was not hiding in the shed, she worked her way toward the next building.

Footsteps behind her caused her to whirl around. "Trevor, I almost shot you," she shout whispered.

He stepped closer to her and spoke in a low voice. "No way was I going to leave you out here alone."

His words brought her consolation. She'd felt so much confusion after their kiss. He seemed to not want to make a big deal of it, so she'd said something to let him off the hook. "It's too dangerous for you. It's the RMK for sure and he has a gun."

"This is the first clear attack on me. We have to get him."

She admired his courage, and his desire to protect her touched her deeply, but this was too risky for him. She leaned close to him. "Go back."

Had the other officers been close enough to hear the shots? Maybe she would get some backup.

Her desire to take in the RMK gave her the courage to keep going.

She took off running, only to find Trevor beside her. There was no time to argue. She had a chance to take in the RMK.

Staying close together, they weaved through the buildings. Without a flashlight, it was hard to see anything in the shadows. The moonlight provided only a small amount of illumination.

They pressed against the stone wall of a round structure and circled it. She stared at the sky in frustration, letting out a heavy breath. He wasn't here. Somehow the RMK had managed to get away without making discernable noise.

"We should head back," said Trevor. "We're not going to flush him out. Maybe he slipped away."

She gripped her gun tighter. If she had had her radio, she could have called more of the team in and cornered him. "I should have handled this differently. I just want to catch him so bad." Her voice came out in a hoarse whisper. "It's best to assume he's still close, waiting to take a shot at us even if we can't hear him. Move with caution."

Using the buildings as cover whenever possible, they worked their way back to the community room, breaking into a full-out run once they were in an open area. When they arrived, the front door was unlocked. They entered to find Isla sitting beside Chase, who was holding an ice pack on his head. Dash was at his feet.

"You're okay." Chase grimaced and adjusted the ice pack. "I've got the others out looking for you."

"We were in pursuit of the RMK," Hannah said. "It was him for sure. I saw his blond hair when his hat fell off."

Chase's voice became solemn. "That means he's here on the grounds." He rose to his feet. "Trevor, you never should have left the building."

Hannah lowered her voice. "This is partially my fault. I thought I was only going to be in my room for a minute. I shouldn't have left my post."

Trevor spoke up. "He was firing shots at the back door. I moved to escape out the front door, and I saw Hannah running. I knew I couldn't leave her out there alone."

"Everything happened so fast, I heard shots, I didn't have time to grab my radio," said Hannah. "I know that I could have handled things better." She stepped toward Chase. "But we almost had him."

Chase touched her arm. "We both played this one poorly. I can't believe I got knocked in the head. I turned away for a second."

"What happened to Dash?"

"We found him tied to a tree. The RMK is very good with dogs. He must have grabbed Dash right after he hit me," Chase said.

"He has to have been watching this place closely. He knew where Trevor was sleeping. He kicked that door open first."

Trevor collapsed in a chair. "When he didn't find me there, he must have looked in the community room window and saw that I was alone."

"We never should have let this happen. Isla, get on the radio, we need to call everyone in for the night. I want two people on shift outside guarding the bunkhouse, one sitting and one patrolling."

"Since this place is so vulnerable, what if Hannah and I returned to my RV with one other person to stand guard."

Chase shook his head. "Like Hannah said, we're being surveilled closely. There is too much danger that the RMK or Weller would see us leave and follow. You wouldn't be any safer at the RV and you'd have less protection."

"But David doesn't have a car," said Trevor. "Hannah would be safer."

Isla spoke up. "Actually, I've been watching the park-police reports and a car was reported stolen about an hour ago not too far from here."

The news was like a jab to Hannah's stomach. That meant David was more mobile.

Chase spoke up. "The smart thing is for all of us to get as much sleep as possible with the guard shifts I set up. I don't want another attack to happen tonight. We'll play offense as well. Whoever is not on guard duty or sleeping will go out to track the RMK. If he's still lurking on the grounds, we'll find him."

Isla moved toward her worktable.

"If we could catch David Weller," said Hannah, "I could be more of a help instead of a liability."

"No one thinks of you that way," Isla responded.

Chase looked at Hannah for a long moment as though he were thinking about something. "I'll escort the two of you back to the rooms."

Chase's tone indicated a level of frustration that Hannah shared. To be this close, to know that he was out there watching them and not to be able to bring the RMK in, was upsetting.

Trevor, Hannah and Captain followed Chase and Dash outside. Hannah said good-night and retreated to her room. After setting her gun on the nightstand, she called Captain over to her.

She rubbed his furry head. "You did good out there tonight, big guy."

Captain licked her hand.

"Now lie down and get some sleep." She put her face close to his. "That's a good boy."

Captain settled on the floor beside her bed. She reached over to turn off the nightstand lamp.

Hannah got into bed fully clothed and pulled the covers up around her. She wondered why Chase had looked at her for a long moment and then not said anything. Did he think she was a liability, or was she projecting her insecurity on him, just like she'd done with Trevor?

She longed for the comfort of his arms around her.

She could feel tears warming the corners of her eyes. From the moment she'd turned onto the causeway to the island, nothing had gone as she'd hoped. She certainly didn't think she would find herself falling for Trevor Gage.

She stared at the ceiling. Captain had risen to his feet. He licked her arm where it was exposed.

She turned to face her partner and rub his ears. "Thanks for always being on my side."

She drifted off to sleep, barely waking when both Isla and Selena came in some time later. Meadow must be on guard duty.

She turned on her side and pulled the blanket around her shoulder, praying that tomorrow would be a more fruitful day and that they all would have a safe night's sleep.

* * *

The next morning, when Rocco had invited Trevor to help cook breakfast, he'd jumped at the chance to keep busy. The smell of sausages filled the air. Trevor got out the orange juice then broke eggs to be scrambled.

Rocco watched the sausages while also pouring pancakes on the griddle. He seemed quite skilled at cooking. Trevor recognized Rocco's last name. There had been a detective named Manelli on the original case, most likely Rocco's father. Catching the RMK was probably as personal to Rocco as it was to Trevor.

The rest of the team slowly shuffled in, grabbing cups of coffee and retreating to the seating area.

Just as breakfast was ready to serve, Hannah appeared at the door and looked into the kitchen. "Rocco, you're going to want to see this since you were the one who transported the pups. Trevor, you might like this. Come see what Isla has set up."

The rest of the team had already gathered around the monitors.

On the screen was a woman Trevor didn't recognize. The woman's dark hair, pulled back in a single braid, offset her caramel-colored skin. She was holding Cowgirl's cinnamon-colored puppy. The other three pups played at her feet in some sort of outdoor pen.

Isla pressed a button on her keyboard. "Liana has a message for all of you."

Liana waved and drew the puppy closer to her face. The puppy licked her cheek as its little legs ran a marathon. "Hey, everyone. I thought you could use some good news. All the puppies are in good health and very active, as you can see." She bent over and picked up the multicolored puppy. Both puppies wiggled in her hands.

Isla leaned forward. "What are the plans for those little guys?"

"We'll start working with them to see if they can be trained as compassion K-9s like their mom." She bent her head toward one of the pups and then looked at the screen as her voice filled with longing. "Any sign of Cowgirl?"

Chase piped up. "She's been spotted several times. It looks like she's being well taken care of."

"I just hope she's recovered soon. I miss her." Liana bent to put the pups down.

Trevor had noticed that the woman's eyes had glazed right before her face went off screen. The atmosphere in the room had grown heavy.

Hannah leaned close to Trevor. "Liana was supposed to adopt Cowgirl. She'd bring her to the Elk Valley PD, where the task force has its HQ, every morning for her work as a therapy dog and then home every night."

Rocco edged toward the screen. "Hopefully soon, Liana, those of us who live in Elk Valley will be back there to see those little guys grow and learn."

"Yes, for sure," said Liana. "I hope you all have a productive day."

"We'll do our best," said Chase.

Liana waved goodbye and managed a smile that didn't quite reach her eyes before the screen went black.

"She's pretty broken up about Cowgirl," said Hannah.

The others nodded in agreement.

"Let's eat breakfast," said Chase. "Whatever it is, it smells good."

After the food was brought out, each of the team members took a seat, as did Trevor.

"I can say grace if you like." Trevor addressed his comment to Chase.

"That would be great," said Chase as he bowed his head and pressed his hands together.

"Lord, we thank You for this day. For the way this team works together and for seeing how healthy and active the puppies are."

Several people laughed.

Trevor continued, "We ask that you protect each and everyone around this table as we work today to bring in these two men who have caused so much havoc. Thank You for this food—please bless and nourish it to our bodies."

Several people said, "Amen."

Trevor raised his head and opened his eyes, allowing his gaze to rest on each of the officers for just a moment. He'd come to a place of respect for the dedication and tenacity he saw in each of these men and women. Their desire to see justice done had restored his faith in law enforcement.

The food was passed around and compliments flowed as people dug into their meals. No one seemed to want to talk about the case.

Isla cleared her throat after setting down her fork on her empty plate. "I have a bit of news that might affect what we do today. It seems that today is the first day of the Kite and Balloon Stampede that's held on the island."

"So that means more people on the island?" Meadow grabbed the last sausage off the serving plate.

"An extra twenty thousand," said Isla. "Most of the activities are at White Rock Bay up north, but I'm sure some people will filter down here."

Chase said, "More traffic too I bet."

"Yes, they launch the balloons off the road sometimes," said Isla. "I imagine things can get pretty backed up."

"Gonna complicate things for us doing our job," said Rocco. "It's a lot easier to hide in a crowd."

"I think we will concentrate our efforts on locating the RMK closer to the ranch for now." Chase pushed back his chair and stood up. "Ian, you stay here with Trevor, Hannah and Isla. The rest of us will search the ranch out of uniform. I don't want to draw attention to ourselves. We'll still have the dogs get a scent off the blankets that were left in the crate with puppies."

"Even though Scout is trained for wilderness terrain, he can handle crowds just fine," said Selena.

The four officers left. Trevor watched through the window of the community room. Already, it looked like there were more people than usual milling through the ranch.

Ian called Lola to his side. "I will be outside patrolling the area close to here." He tapped his radio. "Stay in touch. It looks busy out there."

"I'll be inside with Trevor," said Hannah.

Isla returned to her worktable.

Trevor grabbed his laptop from the bunkhouse and settled down to get some work done. Captain rested on a rug at his feet.

Hannah took a seat opposite Trevor and began reading something on her phone, then rose to look out each window. She sat back down with a heavy sigh.

It was clear she was restless.

Trevor said, "Why don't I get us all something cold to drink?"

"That sounds nice," said Hannah. "I'd take an iced tea if there are any left."

"Isla, you want anything?"

"I'm good," said Isla.

Trevor went to the kitchen and opened the refrigerator. He grabbed the last iced tea and a soft drink.

He thought he heard Hannah say something like "What's that?"

Captain let out a single bark.

When he returned to the sitting area, Isla had risen and pushed back her chair.

Hannah rushed across the room with her hand hovering over her gun.

SEVENTEEN

At the sound of someone rattling the front door, Hannah had risen to her feet. The door burst open.

Two young men tumbled into the community room. They were both dressed in baggy pants and oversize hoodies.

At the sight of Hannah, they put their arms up in the air.

"Whoa," the taller of the two men said.

The second man took a step back. "We were just having a look around the ranch."

"This building is not open to the public," said Hannah. "There should be a sign outside."

"We didn't see any," said the taller man.

"We're sorry," the other man added.

"No problem." She put the hand that had been hovering over the gun at her side. "Sorry to have scared you."

Trevor had risen to stand beside Hannah. "Enjoy your time at the ranch."

The two men left by the door they'd come in by.

"That door should have been locked." Hannah stepped toward it, then examined the door.

"Let me see," said Trevor. He leaned in to have a closer look at the doorknob. "It appears to be broken."

"No surprise there. It's old." She stared at the outside area by the door, not seeing the sign that indicated the bunkhouse wasn't open to the public. She stepped farther out—the sign had been on flimsy wooden post. Someone could have pulled it up.

"Can you fix the lock?"

"Maybe if I had some tools," said Trevor.

She circled the building, looking for the sign. The bunkhouse was close to a thick forest with trails and bird-viewing areas. She spotted at least a dozen people wandering through the trees.

Ian and Lola came around from the other side of the bunkhouse. "Everything okay?"

"The lock on the front door is broken and the sign saying the area isn't open to the public is gone."

"I'll look around for it," said Ian. "You should get back inside."

All the extra people milling through made her nervous. When she returned, Trevor was taking the doorknob apart using a knife as a screwdriver.

"Not sure if this is a good idea," said Trevor. "I'll get it all torn apart and not be able to put it back together. Besides, it looks like the locking mechanism when you twist this—" he pointed to the elevated button in the middle of the doorknob "—won't go down. The knob probably needs to be replaced."

"Neither one of you should be standing here," said Isla. "Let's go inside."

Hannah pushed the door into place behind her. The knob was wobbly. This wasn't good. Not only did it mean the tourist could wander in here, but it was also one less point of protection against the two men. The other door had probably been damaged from the RMK shooting at it, as well. The place was hardly high-security and now it was even less so.

"Isla, can you print up a sign we can put on the door that says the building isn't open to the public?"

"Sure, in just a minute." She lifted her head above her screen. "Want to know what I have been working on?" There was a hopeful lilt in her voice.

Hannah walked over to Isla's worktable. There was a grid on one of her screens with names in the squares. She looked a little closer. "It's a work schedule."

"Remember when you interviewed the HR woman who hired David? She was going to send me the shift schedule to see who worked the most with David and might know something about him that could help us catch him."

Hannah pulled up a chair. "Yes, I remember. What did you find out?"

"David mostly worked alone doing cleanup and maintenance, but there were a few times he did work projects with other park employees. I've got two names for you. Thought you might want to interview them. Won't take but a second to track down their phone numbers."

"Thank you. That could be helpful. I'd like to find out if they know where he stashed that boat."

"Okay, give me a minute." Isla had already put her finger back on the keyboard. She clicked through several screens and then wrote down two phone numbers beside the names she had already written down. Her phone rang. She looked at the phone screen. Her jaw fell. "I have to take this call." Her voice had changed.

She rose and walked into the kitchen, closing the door behind her but leaving it ajar.

Hannah could hear Isla's muffled voice but not any words.

"Wonder what that was about?" Trevor looked up from his laptop.

Hannah shrugged. It had certainly changed Isla's mood.

The call ended but Isla did not return to the seating area. No sound of Isla opening cupboards or turning on a microwave emanated from the kitchen.

Something was wrong. Hannah pushed back her chair. "I'll go talk to her."

She opened the kitchen door. Isla was leaning against the counter with her bent head resting in her hands.

"Hey…" Hannah's voice was soft. "Everything okay?"

Isla lifted her head. Her eyes were filled with tears. "That was the adoption agency." She sniffled. "My application to foster Enzo was turned down."

Hannah felt like a knife had gone through her own heart. Her throat grew tight. "I'm so sorry." She held open her arms and gathered Isla into them.

She held her friend tight while she sobbed.

Isla pulled away and swiped at her eyes. "If you don't mind, I'm going to go lie down for a while." She stepped toward the door but then turned back. "I'll tell the rest of the team when I'm ready. If anyone asks, I don't mind you letting them know."

"Sure, I understand," said Hannah.

"Thank you for being a friend." Isla lifted her head and managed a smile. "I'll get through this. God is faithful, and I will trust his timing in everything."

She admired her friend's steadfast faith. "You'll

get this thing cleared up and have a child to foster. I know you will."

"Thanks. I won't give up hope." Isla left through the back door.

Hannah watched from the window as she headed to the bunkhouse, feeling her own eyes warm with tears.

She returned to the sitting area with a heavy heart.

Trevor was leaning forward on the sofa petting Captain. "Everything all right?" He sat up straighter.

"Isla is really hurting right now. Her application to foster that little boy got turned down."

"What a tough break." Trevor shook his head. "That must have knocked her off her feet."

"She's going to rest for a while." Hannah sat down on the opposite end of the couch from Trevor.

"I got the impression she really wanted that in her life, to have a child."

"She would be a great mom. She has the support of her grandmother to help raise the kid since she's not married and I think she's like me, that she's kind of given up on meeting Mr. Right."

Trevor turned so he was facing Hannah. "What made you give up?"

The question had such weight to it considering her attraction to Trevor. "I just got tired of being hurt by men and living that cycle of hope and disappointment every time it didn't work out when I saw the guy I was dating for who he really was."

She lifted her head and met his gaze. The light in his eyes and the softness of his expression drew her in.

"I'm really sorry that your life has gone that way. You deserved better."

His words were so filled with compassion it was as if she'd let out a breath she'd been holding for years. "What about you?"

"What do you mean?"

"You must be about my age and yet you're not married or with anyone."

He shook his head for a long moment. "Maybe I was punishing myself. Like I didn't deserve that kind of happiness because of what happened ten years ago."

"Self-forgiveness is a thing Trevor." She knew the words were for herself as much as him.

"It would be good to move on, wouldn't it? For both of us." He studied her long enough that his stare made her uncomfortable.

She looked away and stood up, feeling like there should be something more said between them. The conversation made her nervous and afraid. Was she ready to give her heart to this man?

To hide her agitation, Hannah moved over to Isla's work area and grabbed a piece of paper from the printer. "I'll just handwrite a note that says this building is closed off to the public. I don't want to mess with Isla's computers."

After making the sign, Hannah picked up the piece of paper that had the names of the two people who might be able to shed more light on David Weller. She pressed in the first number but got no answer, not even a voice mail.

"Dead end." She shook her head and looked at the piece of paper. "Maybe this woman, Maggie Dunne, will be helpful."

Hannah pressed in the number and waited. A woman's crisp voice came across the line. Hannah asked some preliminary questions and explained that she was with law enforcement. It seemed that Maggie had tried to befriend David because he seemed kind of lonely.

"We talked quite a bit. Over the season, I invited him to a few things that the other employees were doing together. He always had an excuse."

"Do you know if David owned a boat?"

"Oh, sure, just a small motorboat he invited me to go out with him on it. I went, but I was a little concerned that he thought I was interested in him romantically, which was not my intent. I kind of gave him the cold shoulder after that."

"Do you know where he kept his boat when he was on the island?"

"I know when I went out with him, he launched from a little inlet that was a short hike from the Garr Ranch."

She tensed. David liked to have his boat close to where she was right now. Hannah tried to remember if her family had ever docked near the ranch. "You launched the boat from an area by the ranch?"

Trevor raised his head from his laptop, as if what she had said sparked his interest.

"Yes, we left the car in their parking lot just outside the ranch entrance and walked from there."

Now she had an idea of where the docking area might be. Hannah thanked the woman and disconnected from the call.

"That sounded a little more hopeful," said Trevor.

"David might have his boat close to here. I want to go out and search the bay."

"Not alone."

"Maybe Ian and Lola can go with me," she said.

"I'll go with you too. I should not stay here alone anyway."

She pressed her radio. "Ian, are you there?"

His voice came over the line. He sounded out of breath. "Lola picked up a scent. We had to follow it."

"Oh, good. Hope it leads somewhere." Disappointment settled around her. Going down to the water would have to wait.

Hannah disconnected from the radio, crossed

her arms and stared out the window for a long moment. "We're going to have to wait on that. The others might come in for lunch soon."

"Speaking of which. Why don't I go grab us something to eat?"

"Sure, I'm hungry," she said.

Trevor set his laptop on an end table and moved to the kitchen.

Captain rose from the rug where he'd been lying and whined. "I'll take him out real quick to do his business."

Hannah opened the door. Captain ran outside. She stepped across the threshold but stayed close to the building.

Plenty of people milled around the other buildings and in the woods closer to the bunkhouse. Her heart beat a little faster, but she couldn't say why.

Captain had wandered around the corner of the building out of sight.

She stepped away from the community room and called out to her K-9.

Her attention was drawn back to the woods. A man in a hat and sunglasses stepped out from the trees. He looked right at her before turning and disappearing into the trees.

Her throat went tight as she pressed the button on her radio. "Ian, the RMK is here not too far from the bunkhouse. I'm in pursuit."

"I'll get there as fast as we can." Ian's words were jumpy. He must be running.

Meadow and Chase responded that they had been searching not too far from the bunkhouse. "We're on it," said Chase.

Though she did not see him anywhere, Ian would be close by if he and Lola had been hot on the RMK's trail. She ran toward where the RMK had gone. Captain had come back around the building and was a few paces behind her.

She entered the trees where several people were standing by the bird-watching signs, looking up. Her heart raced as she scanned the area. Her eyes were drawn to a man she saw only from the back who was wearing a baseball cap. Though he was not running, he was moving at a steady pace.

She hurried to catch up with him. He disappeared in the thickness of the trees. When she looked over her shoulder, Captain was still behind her.

She pressed her radio. "Ian, where are you?"

"Just got back to the bunkhouse."

It didn't make sense that he was that far away. Hadn't Lola just been on the RMK's scent?

She increased her pace, moving in the direction she'd seen the RMK go. She stepped into an open area. She could see the lake in the distance.

Sensing that someone was behind her, she

whirled around, The man in front of her wore sunglasses and a baseball hat, but it was not the RMK.

David Weller grinned at her. "Did you think I wouldn't see the notices sent out to employees describing the man you've all been looking for?"

She'd been tricked.

She reached for her gun just as he grabbed her arm and yanked it behind her back.

She needed to buy time, to try to break free. "You killed my friend because she looked like your sister?"

"So what if I did." He pushed her arm up higher causing pain to shoot through her body.

She angled side to side trying to get away. Maybe someone would see them struggling before he got her to the water to drown her. Ian might find her if she could only delay long enough. If she could throw him off his game mentally, she might have a chance. "And that man and that woman who looked like your mom and dad. You killed them too."

David grew very still, snaking his free arm across her chest and pulling her close. He hissed in her ear, "I could never live up to Mommy and Daddy's expectations. They ridiculed me. My sister too. They got what they deserved."

It was clear there was no psychological separation between the symbolic parents David had probably killed and his real parents.

He had all but confessed to the killings. She only hoped she would live to testify against him.

When she tried to twist her body, he held her so tightly she could barely move.

She wrapped her leg behind his so she could trip him. They both fell on the ground.

His hands clawed at her as she crawled to get away. He jumped on top of her back with her stomach pressed against the ground.

A hard object hit the side of her head.

She could smell salt in the air and hear Captain barking as she lost consciousness.

EIGHTEEN

Trevor rushed outside when Hannah and Captain hadn't returned after he'd pulled sandwich stuff from the fridge. Ian and Lola raced toward the community room.

Ian pointed. "Hannah is in pursuit of the RMK. Get back inside."

"No way," said Trevor. "Hannah might be in danger."

Ian was already several paces in front of him and probably realized that arguing was pointless. The two men hurried toward the trees. Ian slowed down and looked from side to side. "Something is not right. Lola is not picking up any kind of trail like she did before."

Chase's voice came through the radio. "We're getting close to the community room, but I don't see you."

"We're in the trees," said Ian.

Trevor stopped a man who had binoculars around his neck.

"Did you see a woman in a uniform around here?"

"Yes, just a few minutes ago. She went that way."

Both men ran in the direction that the bird-watcher had pointed.

They came to an open area, where they could see the beach in the distance. Some people were flying kites along the beach. Several people were out on the water in boats of different sizes. A balloon floated over the water.

Trevor shook his head. "Where did she go?"

Then he heard it, a faint but distinct barking.

Lola's ears perked up and she licked her chops.

"That's Captain," said Ian.

They ran toward the sound of the barking, moving around a rock formation that had blocked their view. They found Captain pacing the shore and barking. Trevor scanned the water, allowing his gaze to rest on each boat. A short distance from the shore, a man in a motorboat looked over his shoulder at them. He pulled down his baseball cap lower on his face before increasing his speed. He had something in the boat covered in a tarp.

Alarm bells went off in Trevor's head as he continued to watch the man. Wind caught the corner of the tarp. Trevor thought he saw what looked like a foot, but why would the RMK kidnap Hannah? "I think that's our guy," said Trevor.

Both men glanced along the shore. They needed a boat.

Ian ran toward a man who had just brought a small craft up on the beach. Trevor called Captain and followed Ian and Lola.

"Official police business. I need your boat."

The man stepped away from his boat. "I'll help push it back into the water."

Ian, Trevor and the two dogs jumped in. Once they were in deep enough water, Trevor yanked the pull cord to start the engine, then steered so they were headed in the same direction as the boat that Hannah was probably in.

They passed several other boats but did not see the one they were looking for anywhere.

Trevor steered around a bend. What did the RMK have in mind, anyway? Was this some sort of trap to get at him? If the RMK had been watching at all, he must have noticed how often he and Hannah were together.

Both dogs seemed to be on high alert, with their heads lifted as they sniffed the air.

Trevor shouted above the hum of the boat engine as he scanned the glassy lake. "He's probably going someplace secluded." But where?

Trevor steered closer to the shore and away from the larger boats. Up ahead, he saw trees close to the shore. He headed in that direction. Once around the trees, they entered a C-shaped cove that was framed by a long shoreline on each side covered in rocks and scrubby trees. Up ahead was a man dumping Hannah's body into the water close to the boat. The immobile body barely made a noise as it hit the buoyant water, falling close to the rim of the boat. The man put his hand on Hannah's head and pushed her under.

Ian's hand hovered over his weapon, but he did not draw it. They were still too far away to get an accurate shot. Their boat was already moving at top speed.

The wind blew the man's hat off and Trevor saw the brown curly hair. David Weller.

David's head shot up. He straightened from where he had been bent over holding Hannah's head under water. He started the boat up and sped back toward the open part of the lake, leaving Hannah behind. She floated face-first in the water.

"We have to get to her," Trevor shouted.

Ian looked at the fleeing man and then back at Hannah.

"Take over," said Trevor.

Ian scrambled toward the back of the boat to steer. The boat slowed and drifted in the exchange between the two men as they drew closer to Hannah's floating body.

Trevor shouted the command at Captain he'd heard Hannah use. "Save."

Without hesitation, Captain leaped out of the

boat and paddled toward Hannah. Trevor jumped into the water, as well.

Ian sped off toward the other boat. Swimming in the salt water was arduous. He had to get to Hannah. Captain seemed to take the buoyancy in stride as he got closer to his partner. Still not moving, Hannah had flipped sideways in the water. Captain reached her and tugged on the collar of her uniform to turn her so she was face up, then dragged her toward the shore.

Knowing that Hannah was in good paws, Trevor swam in the direction that Captain went to get to the nearest dry land. Captain brought Hannah ashore with her legs still resting in the water. Trevor reached her seconds later, kneeling over her as water dripped from his hair.

His heart squeezed tight at seeing her pale, lifeless face. She still had a pulse, but she'd probably swallowed water. He began to perform CPR, pressing below her rib cage and then placing his lips on hers. She gurgled. He turned her head to the side. Water spilled out of her mouth.

Still dazed, she looked up at him, reaching her hand to touch his cheek. "Hey," she said.

Her voice made him think of a summer breeze.

He rested his hand on hers. "Hey there. Glad you're okay."

Captain moved in and licked Hannah's forehead. Hannah laughed as she sat up and reached out to touch Captain's dripping wet jowls. "My buddy."

"He saved you."

"I imagine you both worked together," she said.

"I was afraid I'd lost you. I don't know what I would've done if—"

His words were interrupted by the sound of gunfire.

Stunned out of the moment of warmth and connection that had passed between them, Hannah's attention was drawn over Trevor's shoulder as he turned to see the source of the gunfire.

David Weller's boat had run aground at the tip of the peninsula that led into the cove. From his boat, Ian must have fired a shot at him as David neared the rocky shore, where his boat now was. David ran toward the shelter of the rocks and trees.

"He'll have to come back close to here. I can catch him," Hannah said. She tried to push herself to her feet, but her knees buckled.

He reached out to steady her by grabbing her elbow. "You're still weak. Give me your gun."

He was right. In her state, there was no way she could catch up with him. She handed him the gun. Trevor took off running. Captain stayed close to her as she tried to keep up but fell several paces behind him.

As they neared the place where they would collide with David Weller before he took off down the beach, she prayed for more strength.

Trevor got farther ahead of her.

David emerged from the trees, his face red from exertion…or was it rage. Her world seemed to move in slow motion as David turned, saw Trevor, lifted the gun and fired.

Trevor's whole body flung backward as the arm not holding the gun flailed in the air, but he did not fall to the ground. He took aim and fired a shot, then kept running, though his steps seemed much more weighted.

Ian and Lola emerged through the trees as David headed up the beach and dove behind some brush. Lola ran ahead of her partner.

David edged out from behind the bush and fired at Lola. The dog lurched. Her whole body twisted.

Fearing that Lola had been hit, Hannah's heart stopped.

The German shepherd remained standing with her head down. Ian commanded her to stop probably fearing she would be shot if she got closer to the suspect. Trevor had gone out ahead of Ian and Lola.

She saw now that his sleeve was red with blood. Trevor had been hit in the arm that he didn't use to shoot with. A scream got caught in her throat.

She willed herself to go faster, though her muscles felt like mush.

Beyond the brush where David had been hidden was a rocky field. She caught movement, a flash of color. David was running the other way through the rocks.

"That way." She was closer than the other two men, but she could not hope to take on David without a gun. Trevor rerouted himself and headed toward the rocks still holding the gun. Ian and Lola were right behind him. They disappeared behind a large boulder.

Hannah reached the edge of the rocky field with Captain. She heard noise, like one rock crashing into another, and then a gunshot.

Her whole body lurched at the sound. What if Trevor had been shot again? This time fatally?

Captain let out a low growl. Then silence enveloped her. Her heart was still pounding from the exertion of trying to keep up. She stepped toward the rocks. David Weller came out from behind a boulder only yards away from where she was. His back was toward her. She crouched down behind a rock when he glanced her way. When she lifted her head above the rim of the rock, she saw that he was headed toward the boats.

Summoning all the strength she had left, she bolted toward him and leaped in the air, hoping to land on his back. If she missed, he would have time to shoot her. She sailed through the air, hit her target and knocked him down on his stomach. He'd dropped the gun a few feet from his hand.

"Police, you're under arrest." She was so out of breath her voice lacked conviction. She wasn't sure if she'd be strong enough to subdue him for long. Her knees were on the middle of his back and one hand secured his wrist.

David twisted and pushed her off. Just as he dove for her, Trevor emerged from the boulder field.

He landed a blow across David's jaw that caused him to fall backward. He was clearly weakened from his gunshot wound but he held the gun on a stunned David. "It's over."

David sneered. "You look like you're about to fall over."

Ian and Lola came to stand beside Trevor. Ian held his firearm as well, while Lola stood at the ready to take down the suspect.

"Don't even think about it," said Ian. "Put your hands in the air, where I can see them."

David complied though rage was still evident in his eyes. His features were taut, and his teeth showed through his parted lips.

Lola edged closer as Ian moved in to hand-cuff David Weller, who watched the dogs with wary eyes.

Hannah ran toward Trevor. "You've been shot."

He touched his arm. "I think I was just grazed."

Trevor was putting on a brave face, but she had

a feeling he was in pain judging from how blood soaked his sleeve was. "All the same, we need to get you to a hospital."

"I'll take this guy back," said Ian. "If the two of you want to bring his boat in. There is not enough room for all of us in the other boat. He's not going to try anything with Lola close by."

Hannah led Trevor down to the other boat.

They journeyed back up the shore. The rest of the team was there to meet them. Chase ushered Trevor and Hannah back to the bunkhouse and into his car, then they took off to the hospital in Syracuse.

She sat with Chase in the waiting room after Trevor was put in a wheelchair and pushed down a hallway.

Chase leaned his shoulder against hers. "I'm sure he's going to be okay."

"That's what he thought." She still couldn't let go of her fear. What if the wound was worse than it appeared?

Chase rested a hand on her arm. "I can tell you look worried."

"I care about him."

"Care about him? I've seen the way you look at each other. I would say you passed caring about him a while ago."

Her cheeks flushed, and she smiled so widely it almost hurt. "Okay, more than care about him.

I think I love him. He's truly a decent man, everything I ever wanted in a life partner."

"I agree. I wasn't sure from the interviews, but having spent time with him, I see now that he is the real deal."

She let out a breath. It was good to say out loud what she had been thinking for some time. To admit it to herself. She had been so closed off to the idea that any man could be gentle and courageous and loving, that she hadn't been able to believe that Trevor was exactly that.

Chase picked up a magazine that had been lying on the chair beside him and flipped through it. "I wouldn't be surprised if there wasn't another engagement in the task force soon."

"No." She slapped his magazine lightly.

"You never know," he teased.

She knew it was what she wanted. But the big question was how did Trevor feel about her? Their relationship had had so many mixed messages, she still wasn't sure where he stood.

"Engagements are always nice." The smile faded from Chase's face and he got a faraway look in his eyes. Was he thinking about his own life? It seemed that the loss of his wife and baby was the thing that defined him, just as Jodie's death had held a grip on Hannah. Perhaps in the future, Chase would find some measure of happiness, and maybe even love, if all his energy wasn't focused on catching the RMK.

NINETEEN

A spike of pain shot through Trevor's arm as he sat on the couch looking at his phone.

Ian and Isla were in the kitchen. Meadow and Selena had taken their dogs to search the premises, using the scent off the puppy blankets, a reminder that the RMK was still out there, still a threat to his life. It was unclear if the RMK had left the island or was still looking for a chance to come after Trevor.

Rocco muttered something about getting some rest and left the room. Chase and Hannah sat on different couches both looking at their phones.

Earlier, the team had eaten dinner together and raised their water glasses in a toast to David Weller being taken into custody. He would be charged with Jodie's murder as well as attempted murder of Hannah. A case would have to be made against the other two drownings of people who resembled his mother and father. Hannah could testify as to what he had confessed to her before knocking her unconscious.

The sky had grown dark.

After his arm had been treated, they had driven home with little conversation passing between him and Hannah. Not that there wasn't something on his mind. Being shot had changed his perspective on his choices. If the bullet had been a few more inches to the left, he might not be alive. More than anything, he wanted a chance to be alone with Hannah so they could talk.

Hannah rose to her feet. "I think Captain needs to go outside for a bit."

Seeing his opportunity, Trevor also got up. "I'll go with you."

"I don't think that is a good idea," said Chase.

"Selena and Meadow are out there." Trevor gave Chase a steely glare that he hoped communicated that he wanted some time alone with Hannah. "I have lots of protection."

Chase nodded seeming to understand. "Stay close to the buildings."

Hannah had already stepped out the door with Captain when he caught up with her. While Captain wandered around, he came to stand by Hannah. Selena walked by with Scout and nodded in their direction before disappearing around a corner of the building.

"Quite a day, huh?" His mind raced with what to say and how to say it.

"For sure," she said.

"I bet it feels pretty good to close the book on Jodie's death."

"Yes, now I can get on with my life and put my full energy into catching the RMK." She turned to face him. "I know this must be hard for you knowing that the RMK is still out there. You probably hoped he'd be in custody after you took such a risk in staying out in the open."

He stepped a little closer to her. "Being shot has made me rethink some things."

She gazed at him, shaking her head.

"I think maybe I was willing to take such risks because my life didn't matter to me that much, but it does now."

"Are you saying you're willing to go into a safe house?"

"Yes." He stepped closer to her.

"What changed?"

"My life matters to me more now because I want to spend it with you. Hannah, I'm in love with you. I don't want to throw my life away over something that happened ten years ago, and I don't want to be stuck because of it. It's time to look forward, not to live in the past. I can see a future now and I want it to be with you."

"Oh, Trevor. I feel the same way. I just wasn't sure where you stood."

He touched her face. "Hannah, will you marry me?"

"Yes, of course, I will." She gazed up at him.

He bent his head and kissed her. This time there was no doubt what the kiss meant. He wrapped an arm around her waist and drew her close.

After a long moment, she pulled away from the kiss but remained in his embrace. "I don't want to be away from you for even a minute. I'll volunteer as a guard at the safe house."

"Funny way to start out a relationship, but it'll be a great story to tell our kids." He kissed her again.

Captain stood a few feet away from them, watching. His dark coloring blended with the night but is eyes shone.

When Trevor pulled free of the kiss, he saw that Chase, Isla and Ian had all come outside.

"About time you two realized what you are to each other," said Chase.

Selena and Meadow had drawn closer, as well. The whole team applauded and spoke words of congratulations.

Trevor embraced Hannah and kissed her to another round of applause. He relished holding the woman he wanted to spend his life with.

* * * * *

If you enjoyed this story, don't miss
Search and Detect
the next book in the
Mountain Country K-9 Unit series!

Baby Protection Mission
by Laura Scott, April 2024

Her Duty Bound Defender
by Sharee Stover, May 2024

Chasing Justice
by Valerie Hansen, June 2024

Crime Scene Secrets
by Maggie K. Black, July 2024

Montana Abduction Rescue
by Jodie Bailey, August 2024

Trail of Threats
by Jessica R. Patch, September 2024

Tracing a Killer
by Sharon Dunn, October 2024

Search and Detect
by Terri Reed, November 2024

Christmas K-9 Guardians
by Lenora Worth and Katy Lee, December 2024

Available only from Love Inspired Suspense
Discover more at LoveInspired.com

Dear Reader,

I hope you enjoyed getting to know Hannah and Trevor as they fell in love and came up against dangerous situations. Both characters have been affected by traumatic events in their past, to the point where they are stuck, unable to move on, or see a bright future. All of us in one way or another allow our past to define us and determine the choices we make. It doesn't have to be something as traumatic as the death of a friend. Sometimes it's something mean a teacher or relative said to us about our ability to draw, write or play music. Or a person called us a name that we began to believe was true. All those things can cause us to be trapped. The verse in Isaiah 43:19 says, "Behold, I will do a new thing." With God's help, we can have a fresh start and let go of the things in the past that we let define us and keep us stuck. I love to hear from readers. You can learn more about me and my books at www.sharondunnbooks.net.

Sincerely,
Sharon Dunn